COSCOM
ENTERTAINMENT

ALSO BY A.P. FUCHS

Blood of My World Trilogy

Discovery of Death
Memories of Death
Life of Death

Undead World Trilogy

Blood of the Dead
Possession of the Dead

THE AXIOM-MAN™ SAGA
(listed in reading order)

Axiom-man
Episode No. 0: First Night Out
Doorway of Darkness
Episode No. 1: The Dead Land
City of Ruin
Of Magic and Men (comic book)

OTHER FICTION

A Stranger Dead
A Red Dark Night
April (writing as Peter Fox)
Magic Man (deluxe chapbook)
The Way of the Fog (The Ark of Light Vol. 1)
Devil's Playground (written with Keith Gouveia)
On Hell's Wings (written with Keith Gouveia)
Zombie Fight Night: Battles of the Dead
Magic Man Plus 15 Tales of Terror
Undeniable

ANTHOLOGIES (as editor)

Dead Science
Elements of the Fantastic
Vicious Verses and Reanimated Rhymes: Zany
Zombie Poetry for the Undead Head

NON-FICTION

Book Marketing for the
Financially-challenged Author

POETRY

The Hand I've Been Dealt
Haunted Melodies and Other Dark Poems
Still About A Girl

Go to
www.canisterx.com
&
www.undeadworldtrilogy.com

BLOOD OF MY WORLD

Memories of Death

A. P. Fuchs

COSCOM ENTERTAINMENT

WINNIPEG

ISBN 978-1-926712-83-3

PUBLISHED BY COSCOM ENTERTAINMENT
www.coscomentertainment.com
Text set in Garamond; Printed and bound in the USA
COVER ART BY C.J. HUTCHINSON

For Honey

Memories of Death

Glass In Between

My heart is intrinsically tied to yours
Hammered up
Against the wall
I see you
You see me
A wall of glass in between

You reach out to me
Your palm ready to receive
My fingers match yours
We touch
Glass in between

If the wall was ours
We'd break it down
But others build it
Stand in our way

Why did you let them?
Why did I let them?
I've betrayed you
You've betrayed me

I love you
Though there's this glass
Glass in between

1

IT HAD BEEN three weeks since Zach Mohansen had been reborn into the world of the undead, since he'd become a vampire. In that time his new family—his mother, Mira; his father, Rain; his brother, Wil; and his sister, Cassie—had taught him much about his new life and what it meant. Rain had been especially helpful, taking him under his wing and showing him how to use his new abilities. Mira, it seemed, was keen on hunting for blood and, out of all his family members, was present most when Zach went out at night to feed.

It was the feeding that was the most life-changing for Zach, for with each new victim came an onslaught of that person's memories, and with each flash of a life now gone, it triggered memories of his own before he became one of the undead.

Now, around four in the afternoon, and wandering the rows of Eagle Park Cemetery, Zach wondered if it would be appropriate to contact his old family. The dark overcast sky above reminded him of when he was a child and played a baseball game in similar weather. The game eventually had been rained out, but before it was, his team was leading 5-to-3. Though it was day, the light filtering through the clouds didn't bother him as much as it used to. His skin still tingled with heat, like dipping your hands in a sink of hot water, but it was manageable. True daylight, however, would set him on fire. When he asked Rain why this was so, his father didn't have an answer, but did say it was due to spiritual matters Zach wasn't yet mature enough to understand.

But solemn reflection wasn't the sole reason Zach was out amongst the gravestones. It was that girl, the one who called him by name three weeks ago during her mother's funeral. It was the same girl that was in the flashbacks after his first kill. He didn't know her name, but he knew he needed to find out.

If the past was any indicator, she would be here in the cemetery today, as she had been for the past three weeks around this time. Zach had seen her every time she appeared, but kept himself hidden amongst the tombs, his mother's warning to not mingle with the humans his main reason for doing so.

I hope she shows up today, he thought. She would come to pay respects at her mother's gravesite, then would walk the cemetery lines for a half hour or so before leaving. *She seemed to know me, but more so, I seem to know her. Just wish I knew who she was.* Memories that activated after feeding sometimes revealed her face: this girl laughing, crying, walking the halls at a school. *I need to talk to her.*

He positioned himself close to the columbarium that contained the girl's mother's ashes, hid behind a tree, and waited.

Rose got off the bus at the stop near the gates of Eagle Park Cemetery, her heart pounding inside her chest. These daily visits weren't healthy, she knew. It wasn't easy going up to her mother's grave and saying good-bye again and again. Her father, Marcus, had sternly warned her he didn't want her going to the cemetery without him. Ever since she had encountered what he said was a vampire the day of her mom's funeral, Eagle Park was strictly off limits.

"Especially," he had said, "if it was indeed Zach you saw. If he is now one of them, he is more dangerous than you could ever know. Until you are fully trained, I do not want you setting foot in Eagle Park Cemetery. Am I clear?"

She had nodded, her fingers crossed behind her back as if that made it all okay. In the weeks since, she'd come to terms with her father's second job outside of his real estate practice, and each evening was filled with stories of past missions, how she had been raised in a home of slayers without ever knowing it, and what it meant to be on the path to becoming one herself. Right now most of the information shared was overview stuff, but a few things were revealed in depth: old archive newspapers detailing grisly deaths where the victim had been bled dry; missing persons cases; slayer history and chain of command.

"It will be a life of secrets," her father had told her, "but do not mistake these secrets for lies. A slayer is more than just a man or woman's occupation. It is their life, a calling to become that which this world so desperately needs. It is not to be taken lightly." Time was taken each day to get in shape and learn combat maneuvers and weapon control. It would take a long time to master, but her dad said there'd be a lot of on-the-job training as well.

"Nothing can replicate firsthand experience," he had said.

Rose entered the cemetery and made her way to her mother's grave. *Secrets or not,* she thought, *I need time to think, to process, to grieve.* Her father didn't seem to understand that. Not only was she still working through her mother's death, she was also dealing with learning who her father really was, and also coming to terms with what that meant for her own life. Any hopes and aspirations she had under the veil of normalcy were now of no consequence. Instead, revelation had changed the course of her life forever.

She walked up to her mother's grave. "Hi, Mom." She took a deep breath and wiped away the tears that had formed at the corners of her eyes.

◆ ◆ ◆

How do you explain what it's like to see someone you don't know, yet feel like you were once part of their world all the same? It was impossible, Zach figured. The most he could come up with was what he sensed when seeing this girl who lived on the *third tier* of what made him who he was. The first, was his intellect, the realm of thought, choices and information. The second was his feelings and the emotions that ran through him, and even though undead, there was a constant *feeling* that ran through him: he was numb. Just the way it was.

The third tier was where this girl lived inside him: his heart, something separate from his mind and emotions. It was deep inside where something simply *was* and not determined by thought or feeling. It was a place of truth, of fact, of utter *isness*.

This girl had somehow gotten herself a place there, and today Zach was determined to find out how.

Slowly, he moved along the trees, speeding from behind one to the next, until his path formed a semi-circle that came up in behind the girl. Even now, standing some fifteen feet away behind a tombstone, the way she looked from the back seemed familiar and a part of him wanted to speed up to her, wrap his arms around her and hold her.

But you don't know her, he told himself. *At least, I don't remember knowing her.*

Looking at her from behind wasn't the same as looking at her face. From the front, she seemed more *human* and altogether real. Back here, she reminded him of the other women he'd snuck up on, only to snap their necks to the side and start feeding.

Cautiously, he set one foot in front of the other and walked toward her.

She was crying, her sobs soft, her words whispers, but to his radar-sharp ears, they were as loud as a thunderclap.

"I just wish I knew what to do," she said. "Dad wants me to help him. I don't think I can. Especially if what he said about Zach is true."

Zach stopped his advance when he heard his name. *What about me is true? Does she know what happened to me before my mother found me? Am I even the Zach she's talking about?* He was now right behind her, the scent of her hair traveling through his nose and straight to his heart, sending the sensation of memory rushing into his mind but unable to fully form.

He stepped back so he was an arm's length away. *I don't even know what to say or how to begin. Oh, Rose . . .* His eyes went wide at the realization that he knew her name. How or why, he didn't know, but the name just came to him, surfaced in his mind naturally.

"Rose?" he said softly.

The girl's shoulders went up with a jolt; with a yelp, she turned around, a hand to her chest. "Za—" She cleared her throat. "Zach?"

He nodded, a jumble of words on his tongue but kept behind the locked doors of his lips.

Tears welled up in her eyes and rolled down her cheeks. "Zach, how are you . . . is it you?"

"Yes," he said softly. It was all he could manage. So she *did* know him.

She straightened and kept her eyes fixed on his. It seemed she was looking for something in his face, but he couldn't tell what. Yet that look of heartache in her eyes made him wonder if he had done something wrong.

With short, choppy steps, she came up to him then wrapped her arms around him. "I've missed you. I've missed you so, so much. Where have you been? Everyone's looking for you. I thought you were . . . I mean . . . are you okay?"

"I'm fine," he said.

She slightly pulled away, her cheek brushing against his. Her eyes searched his, then she rose up on her toes and put her warm lips upon his own. She pressed her face into his, as if she'd been waiting to kiss him for years. Zach didn't know what to do: if he should kiss back or pull away, but he didn't have to make that decision. She pulled away first.

"Your mouth is so cold," she said.

"I know."

"You need to say something more than two words."

"I don't know what to say." *You know me, but I don't know where you and I met.* Of all things, he said, "Your name is Rose, right?"

She shook her head slowly. "What? Yes, of course it is. What's the matter with you?" Her eyes rose to his forehead. "Were you hurt? Did something happen and you . . . you don't remember and you've been lost this whole time?" Her words cracked at the end.

"I am lost," he said. "And something did happen."

Rose put her arms around him again. "What?" Fear was in her voice.

"I don't know where to begin." Darkness and anger

swelled up within him, the desire to feed beginning to take hold. He had to push the feeling way down. If this girl could provide further clues to his past, he had to keep her alive.

"Just start with whatever you remember." She squeezed him tighter. "Oh, I can't believe you're here. It was you on the day of my mom's funeral, right?"

"Your mother's—I'm sorry."

"Thanks. And I'm so glad I saw you that day. It all happened so fast that all I remember is you coming up to me, me hugging you and then you suddenly being gone. A part of me wondered if it was a ghost. Then my dad said—" She stopped.

"He said?"

"Doesn't matter. You're here now. I've missed you like crazy. I love you so much, Zach."

Her words didn't affect him, though he understood what she meant. There was something inside him that was connected to this girl, too, but it wasn't love. He didn't know what that felt like and couldn't remember if he ever did.

Not far from where they stood, Zach caught a glimpse of something behind one of the mausoleums. He searched further, eyeing the side of the above-ground crypt where he thought he saw something black flicker in and out of sight.

When he saw his mother's face, he quickly said, "I have to go."

"Go? Go where? Please, don't. Please stay with me. You can't go. We need to go home. You need to see your family."

My family? He realized she meant the human one. If he left her now, they'd be notified he was here in Eagle Park. He thought about killing her. Feeding on her blood would no doubt bring an onslaught of memories and, perhaps, fill the gaps that still remained.

He let the darkness swell inside and begin to transform him so he could sink his teeth into her and bleed her dry.

His mother sped from behind one mausoleum to the next, coming closer to them. If she found them, she would ensure this girl would die. But what if Rose could tell him more about himself if left alive?

Mira drew nearer, keeping out of sight. Zach had watched her enough these past few weeks to become proficient in tracking her movements.

He pushed the darkness back down, and felt the bones in his face realign back to the way they were.

"Rose?" he said.

She nestled her head against his breast. "Yes?"

"Hold on."

Zach's feet left the ground, taking her with him.

IT HAD TO be a dream, Rose thought. Zach was supposed to be dead, and then here he was, his arms wrapped tightly around her, their bodies soaring higher and higher into the sky.

Her heart racing, she looked past their feet to the world below, the city and surrounding suburbs nothing more than a grid of tiny houses, buildings and little black dots moving up and down gray lines.

Did I die? she wondered. *Is Zach my guide to the netherworld? But that would mean he's dead, too. The cemetery . . .* It was possible. Cemeteries weren't the safest places, and if everything her father had told her over the past few weeks was true, cemeteries held other threats besides the undead: grave robbers, muggers, Goth psychos conducting bizarre rituals.

Zach.

She took in his pale complexion and the cool gaze in his eyes.

"Don't be afraid, Rose," he said. "I have you."

At first she didn't understand what he meant, but then a moment later realized she was shaking, quivering with fear. It was all rushing in to meet her: a whole new world, with a whole new meaning.

Zach scooped her up in his arms and she felt more secure with something now under her legs. He took her high above the city before slowing his flight and descending down to the Radisson Hotel's rooftop.

When her feet touched down, she barely had the

strength in them to keep standing. She remained in his arms, just simply needing to be held by him after all this time.

"Rose," he said, "I've missed you." Zach squeezed her close.

"I thought you didn't know me," she said.

"Me, too. What I said just came out." He pulled away from her, took a step back, and looked her up and down. "It's . . . confusing for me. But with you here, it seems like I'm . . . connected to something I've forgotten."

She arched an eyebrow.

"It's hard to explain," he said.

She pressed her lips together, then said, "I believe you, though."

"You do?"

"I do. But I also don't know what to do or what to say. Do you remember me at all?"

He gazed off to somewhere past her. "I know your face. It comes to me when I . . . . . It comes to me in flashes, and every time it does, it's very familiar."

"What happened? Where did you go? I've been worried sick about you for months."

His eyes met hers, his gaze cool. "I don't know where I went or even completely what you mean by that. What I do know is my life now is different than the one you seem to know."

That much is obvious. You can fly! She didn't want to let on that she knew what he was. Rose wanted to see if he'd offer that information himself. She put a hand on her pocket, verifying her cell phone was there. If worse came to worse, she had her father on speed dial. Yet, this was *Zach* and even though she knew she should be afraid of him for what he had become, the fact that it *was* him took that edge off. She hated straddling between wanting to stay and wanting to run, and up here, where could she run to? It was like those dreams where she followed the scary man that hunted her out of pure intrigue instead of listening to commonsense.

"I can tell something's different about you," she said, "aside from the, um, flying, of course."

"About that . . . I'm different now. That's why I can't remember you as much as I should."

Her heart ached at the thought he had forgotten about them and all they meant to each other, but she also knew it wasn't his fault. Her father said sometimes those who are turned into the undead lost the memory of their former life for a while.

She took a small step back and hoped he didn't notice. "How did we get up here?"

He looked at her as if she should already know the answer.

"What I mean is, how did *you* get us up here?"

He glanced at his feet. "We flew, Rose. *I* flew."

"But, Zach . . . people can't fly."

"I can," he said. "I'm not . . . I'm not human anymore." The look on his face was that of a child admitting to something they did wrong.

So it's true, she thought. Tears welled up in her eyes. This meant Zach had died and had come back as a creature her father said was dangerous and unholy.

She turned away from him so he wouldn't see the tears roll down her cheeks.

"Rose?" he said.

She didn't reply, and instead wiped her eyes.

"Rose," he said, then was suddenly behind her, "I'm a vampire."

H

Mira stood with Rain in the center of their crypt.

"Do you know when they'll be coming back?" Rain asked.

"No," she said.

Wil and Cassie bickered at the far end of their underground home. Cassie reached out to touch Wil and he growled and snapped his teeth at her as if trying to bite her hand off.

"Kids!" Mira said. "Your father and I are talking."

The two younger ones looked at her, then whispered back and forth, arguing about something. Mira didn't care so didn't listen in as to what.

"I'm sure he remembers her," Rain said. "I've noticed over the past week that Zach's been detached. I can see the images processing behind his gaze. I've looked into his thoughts. He's trying to remember himself." He took her hands in his. "We need to let him be with her for a time. He needs to get close."

"We won't say a word. Should he ever bring her here, we've never met her."

"And when the time is right, we will make our move."

"Agreed, my love. Agreed."

◆ ◆ ◆

Zach sensed the darkness creeping in around him. Between trying to ignore the heat on his skin despite the clouds, and trying to recall what he could about Rose, it would be all too easy to let the darkness take over and for him to bite her. He checked his hands. They were already spackled with red, burning blisters.

She hadn't said anything since he told her what he was. She just stood there, facing away from him, arms crossed.

"Rose?" he said. "Did you hear me?"

She nodded. "I'd say that you're joking," she said, "but only because you flew us up here do I believe you."

"Do you hate me for it?"

She put her face in her hands for a moment before pulling them away and straightening.

The sound of her blood flowing through her veins made him want to reach out and grab her and sink his teeth into her neck. *You can't!* he thought. *She's your link to your old life. You need to keep her alive until you remember everything.*

He closed his eyes and focused on setting the darkness rising within at bay.

"I'm just . . . amazed," she said, "that you're real. That, um, vampires are real."

He heard her heart skip a beat and assumed it was because of the reality sinking in. She didn't seem the type to lie to him. "Yes, we are."

"We?"

He said too much. How she set him so at ease, he didn't know. "I've become what I've become, and the life I now lead is one filled with wonder."

"Do you . . . drink blood?" she asked. "Like in the movies?"

He glided around in front of her and searched her eyes for the reply she wanted to hear. *Please say no,* he heard her think. But he couldn't lie to her even though he wanted to. Not Rose. He could never lie to Rose.

The word was out of his mouth before he had a chance to restrain himself. "Yes."

She closed her eyes as if to bite back tears. When she opened them, she said, "I want to go now."

He nodded. It was over. "As you wish."

◆ ◆ ◆

Zach floated Rose down to the alley running alongside the hotel, out of sight of the busy city streets around it.

As much as she wanted to spend more time with him, she needed time to process what he told her and, maybe, discreetly ask her father more questions about the undead without letting on she confirmed Zach was one of them.

Her feet touched the ground and being at street level never felt so good. "Thanks."

"You're welcome." Zach eyed his hands. They were orangey-red; so were his cheeks, blisters dotting his skin.

"Are you okay?"

"I'll be fine. I have to go." His words were short, curt and to the point. Whatever tenderness she had experienced from him on the rooftop was now gone.

"Okay," she said, reciprocating his tone. Now that they were in the alley, she wanted their time together to be over. It was just too much.

"Rose?"

"Yes?"

"I hope I didn't scare you."

"You did, but . . . it's not your fault. I don't think it is, anyway."

"I don't know about that," he said. His face and body blurred, and the next moment he was gone.

If it wasn't for her being downtown, she might have

questioned the whole experience, yet here she was, out of the cemetery and in the city.

I just hope you're okay, Zach, she thought. *Maybe in time we can figure this all out.*

She pulled her cell phone out of her pocket, her heart hammering inside her chest. "Just be calm, just be calm," she said and dialed her father. When he answered, she said, "Dad? I need a ride."

G

Marcus DIDN'T HAVE to be a mind-reader to know Rose's thoughts were elsewhere. She sat beside him in the passenger seat, gazing out the window, one hand on her lap, the other pressed up against her cheek, elbow on the passenger door.

"How was school?" he asked, knowing how cliché it sounded. It was all he could bring himself to say, though. He couldn't just outright ask if she missed her mom.

"Fine," she said, and kept her gaze out the window.

"Anything particular you want for supper?" He glanced her way. Rose just shook her head.

"Going to have to keep it simple. Maybe Chinese take-out. We need to go to *the house* and get ready for tonight."

"I miss going home," she said softly.

"You do?"

"What do you think? Of course, I do. It's our *home*, remember? We spend so much time at the other place that *that* is beginning to feel like home."

"I'd think that's a good thing."

"As if," she said.

"It needs to be." He spoke before he meant to.

She shot him an incredulous look. "What's that supposed to mean?"

"It means," he said, then lowered his voice, "you need to be comfortable with what we Jordans do. You need to understand where our loyalties are."

She looked back out the window. "I do

understand . . . but I—I miss the way things used to be, too."

"So do I," he said.

"But the way I remember them—with you, Mom, us—is different than how you remember them. You and Mom snuck around all this time and didn't tell me. Then you drop the news you're vampire slayers and I'm just supposed to run with that?"

"Where's all this coming from? I thought you had accepted that our lifestyle comes at a certain price, but as a result, we're also afforded certain liberties as well." Marcus sighed. "You're not having second thoughts, are you?"

It was a while before she replied. "I don't know."

◆ ◆ ◆

Zach flew through the air, rejuvenated after seeing Rose, his vampiric body even more flooded with vigor. She had tapped into a secret part of him that hadn't yet manifested itself since his rebirth. Being with her today brought back a flood of memories—to a point. He sensed the memories in his mind, but when he tried to think of them, all he saw were red waves against a black canvas.

He took off into the gray clouds, careful not to emerge above them in case the sun shone bright up there. He just wanted to be here, in this void of gray nothingness, with no distractions, the pain from the heat on his skin a tool to cut him off from everything but his thoughts.

He needed to let the memories come.

They had to.

Zach stopped his flight and hovered in the air, relaxing his body against the air currents, riding them but still maintaining control.

"Rose," he whispered. "Rose." He closed his eyes. *Help me remember.* Though he couldn't read her thoughts nor place his own with her this far away, he still felt her in his . . . heart.

Something wasn't right. Emotion was dead to him. Why was this happening? Though his heart did not beat, a tingle of electric vibration ran through it every time he thought of her. Some kind of weird bodily reaction to meeting her? A new side effect of a memory surfacing?

Zach thought about asking his mother what this was, but she would throw a fit if she knew he had been with a human and not slaughtered them.

Red, wavy lines on black canvas, continuously floating past his mind's eye. The lines rose up and down, their speed increasing with each passing moment. The lines began to curve until they became a smoky spiral against the black, turning and twisting and reforming themselves until . . . flower petals burst before his eyes and floated down against the black like snow.

The black and red faded, revealing a soccer field in a schoolyard. Zach was suddenly at ground level, walking, something holding his hand. He looked down to see delicate female fingers intertwined with his own. He followed the fingers to the hand, up the arm, past the shoulder and neck to Rose's beautiful face. She wore a white sweater, a red shirt beneath and blue jeans. He wanted to wrap his arms around her and pick her up. And he did. He scooped her up by the waist, brought her into the air, then slowly lowered her back to the ground. Rose landed with her hands upon his shoulders, her hazel eyes looking into his.

"I can't believe this is happening," she said.

"Me neither," he replied, the words coming out as if

he was following a script. "Never thought we'd—"

"Oh, don't rub it in." She smiled.

He did, too. "What I meant was I never thought we'd—meaning 'us'—would get to the place, you know, where things just really seem to *fit.*"

"I know what you mean."

"It's like a whole new part of me has been opened, one that I kind of sensed was there but didn't really give a good look at. But you . . . you just make everything all right." He took her hands off his shoulders and gently held them by his chest. "You took my heart, broke it into a million pieces, fused it with passion, then put it back together again, better and stronger." Tears welled in his eyes. "I love you, Rose, with all my heart."

She smiled just a little, then squeezed her eyes shut as a tear rolled down her cheek. When she opened them, she met his gaze and said, "I love you, too. You're everything to me."

Zach's heart ached. He let go of her hands and placed his on her hips. He gave them a gentle squeeze as he drew her in closer, then he closed his eyes and kissed her, losing himself in her completely. His heart was now hers, and he held Rose's as well.

Their lips moved together, each brush of their flesh like electricity racing through their mouths and burning themselves into each other.

I love you, Rose. Forever. Everything went black and Zach opened his eyes. He was still in the clouds high above the earth, his heart aching.

◆ ◆ ◆

Rose stood outside at the rear of the Slayer House, gazing up into the night sky, wondering if Zach was somewhere up there flying around. Seeing him today, finding out he was—alive?—and what he had become was like having a huge weight lifted off of her.

But he's dead, she thought. *Kind of.* She knew vampires were no longer of the living, but the way they moved and talked could make a person think otherwise.

"You can't love a dead person," she told herself. *Is there a way to get Zach back to normal? Is there a cure?* Maybe. She'd have to figure out a casual way to ask her father about it. "I hope so."

"Rose?" Her father peeked out the back door. "It's time."

She glanced up into the sky one last time, then said, "Coming."

Tonight she would slay a vampire for the first time.

She prayed Zach kept his distance.

5

ZACH PACED THE crypt, eyes to the floor. Every few steps he'd rise above the ground then float back down again.

"Zach, dear, please stop that. You're giving me a headache," Mira said as she occupied her hands darning one of Rain's old coats.

"We don't get headaches, you know that."

"It is a figure of speech, or have you forgotten that, too?" Her tone conveyed it was meant not in scorn, but as a genuine inquiry as to the severity of his memory loss.

"No, I remember. Was just surprised to hear you say what you did."

She lifted the coat off her lap and held it before her, examining her work. "Are you ready for tonight's outing?"

"Yes." *Each time I drink, I feel like I'm being put back together, each memory another piece to the puzzle that is me.* And though feeding was a priority right now, he desperately wanted to see Rose again. He just didn't know how soon after seeing her he should, well, see her.

"I've never seen you this nervous before," Mira said. "Is something wrong?" Her words were almost monotone in delivery.

Zach finally stopped pacing midair and floated to the floor. "No," he said. *I just miss her, is all.* He stopped himself before he thought any further. He didn't want his mother to know he had spent time with a human in the way that he had. Hopefully she hadn't read his mind just now.

Mira folded up the coat and laid it neatly on top of Rain's coffin.

Zach pointed to it. "Is Father coming?"

"No. He and the others are already out there."

"Why didn't he invite me?"

"You were sleeping when they went out and he didn't want to wake you."

He thought for a moment. "Are we hunting together tonight, Mother?"

"Would you like to?"

I want to see Rose. Can't do that if she is around. "I would love to," he said, "but I also need to practice hunting on my own. I hope you understand."

She smiled sweetly. "I do." She held out her hand to him. "Come, let us find something to eat."

Zach took her hand as if about to take her in his arms for a dance, and led her up the crypt's steps to the entrance. He let go of her hand once at the top and opened the door. They passed through the mausoleum to the cemetery. The night air was warm, and thick with humidity.

When Zach stepped out further, a quick image flashed before his eyes, one of a night similar to this one, out in the woods. The crackle of a bonfire, a man sitting across from him holding a stick with a marshmallow on the end. The man's features were obscured by the dancing flame, but it was evident the man was smiling at him.

"Honey?" Mira asked, a hand to his shoulder. "Everything okay?"

"I'm fine. Just saw something."

"What?"

"Nothing. Just an image."

"Want to share?"

Why is she being so nosy? he thought. He understood it was her job to help him ease into the vampire life, but he had been one of the undead for several weeks now and yearned for some space.

"No, I'm fine, thank you," he said.

"Okay. Be careful. Choose your meal wisely. Ensure no one sees you. If there's trouble, fly away. Fly back here."

"I will," he said, and looked up into the sky. It was clear, the moon out in full, the stars dotting the black-purple of the night in sparks of light.

Zach's feet left the ground and he twirled himself in the air as he ascended. With each foot of height gained, the freer and better he felt. Up here, it was his own little world, with no input from anybody else.

"Rose needs to see this," he said. "So beautiful."

He stopped his ascent and hovered in the air. Cars moved up and down the streets far below in streaks of red and yellow. The lit roads and lights from homes created a mosaic of gold and black.

Darkness crept in around his vision and began to fill his heart. Every other sense subsided as a boiling rage swelled within and overtook his mind and will.

The sharp pain of bone shifting against bone and rubbing against skin set his face on fire as his muscles and bones realigned themselves to allow for feeding. His teeth grew sharp against his tongue and already he could taste the blood he was about to let flow down his throat.

Tearing through the sky, Zach searched the dark below, his eyes able to scan the streets as if he was down there himself. His eyes also magnified the available light so everything was bright and clear behind a veil of red and yellow.

A girl walked the street below, one with a white

hooded sweatshirt and pink jeans. Her blonde hair bounced with each step as she made her way down the street, not walking on the sidewalk but sticking to the curb instead.

Would she be missed? She appeared only seventeen or eighteen years old, and still had the glimmer in her eye of someone who had their whole life ahead of them, and the hope of a happy ending.

The anger surrounding Zach's heart grew darker and more intense, its desire to kill propelling his body through the air at a terrible speed. Quickly, he was not far from street level. As fast as he could, he snapped out his arms and snatched the girl from the street and flew her high into the sky.

She shrieked the higher they went, her arms and legs kicking and flailing.

To keep her still, Zach wrapped his legs around hers and jerked his legs back, snapping her knees. She howled. Using his legs to hold her, he shot out his hands and grabbed each of her arms and broke them at the elbows. The girl screamed in pain. Zach adjusted his grip and held her around the chest. Mouth open wide, he clamped down around her neck and sunk his teeth in. Blood squirted inside his mouth, its warmth hitting the cool flesh of his inner cheeks and the back of his throat.

The girl stopped screaming and instead gasped for air. Zach held her tighter and sucked on her neck, pulling her life away from her. Euphoria rocked him to the core and his body went rigid with intense, orgasmic pleasure.

Arcing backwards, he inverted himself and sped toward the ground, still clinging to the girl's body and drinking her blood. He adjusted his flight path, twisted himself over, and flew just above the tops of the trees lining the Red River. With one final pull on the girl's neck, he sucked out another gulp of blood, then released her body into the trees below. Her body fell through the canopy and his hypersensitive hearing heard the thud of her body hitting the leaf-ridden ground. She wouldn't die; she would turn.

Zach took off into the night, readying himself for the girl's memories to fill him.

6

Rose's heart beat hard in her chest. Tonight all she'd been preparing for would come to fruition. Under the ever-watchful eye of her father, she would end a vampire's life and remove their threat from the earth.

What if the one I slay tonight is Zach? she thought. She still hadn't told her father about his transformation. She knew that if he did find out, he would keep her under lock and key until he slayed Zach himself. *I hope not. I don't even really want to kill one of them tonight, not after the kindness Zach showed me. They can't* all *be bad, can they? If Zach didn't harm me, wouldn't that mean that maybe there were others who found sustenance in something other than humans?*

"We're here," Marcus said, and pulled into an empty spot at The Forks, a place in the city where the Assiniboine and Red Rivers met. Now a tourist attraction, one with an indoor market, old train, a couple of clubs and a dock, it was a hub of activity. Even late at night when the grounds were closed, late-night couples would stroll the path along the riverbank anyway, hold hands and say I love yous. Isolated like that, under the cover of darkness, made them easy pickings for the undead.

Tonight the grounds were already shut down, only one other car in the parking lot. Rose suspected it belonged to either a janitor or security guard.

She and her father got out of the SUV, rounded to the trunk, and upon opening it began to arm themselves with tools for tonight's hunt. Rose girded her waist with a belt lined with silver stakes, their weight heavy enough she had to tighten the buckle so the belt wouldn't fall off her waist. On her back she sheathed a machete.

Her father was already armed and had his long, black overcoat on when she turned to him. He closed the trunk of the vehicle, locked it with a press of a button on the remote on his keychain, and guided her by the arm past the indoor market and toward the steps leading down to the gravel path along the river.

"For now, stay beside me," Marcus said. "Should we discover one of them, I want you to get behind me and follow my lead. Understood?"

I guess. Oh, Zach, don't be here. Not tonight. "Yes," she said.

The two made their way to the pathway, headed right, and started their stroll down the dimly-lit river walk.

First rule of the hunt was silence, so Rose kept her mouth shut. She scanned the water on her left, wondering if the undead were able to swim. She didn't see why not but it was something never covered in her lessons. Her father seemed to have his eyes set on the trees and bushes to the right. Up ahead was a bridge that arched over the river and pathway, leading to the street running perpendicular to them.

Marcus put a hand on her back. "Smell that?" he whispered.

Rose sniffed the air. A subtle scent of rotting meat hung on the wind. It wasn't overt, but enough to catch your attention if you were looking for it. "Yeah."

"Get ready."

They continued down the path and started under the bridge.

Two shadows dropped from beneath the bridge's rafters, landing on the ground securely, as if they'd only jumped off a small step instead of coming down thirty feet.

One of the shadows—a man in a black turtleneck and

black jeans—was near Rose's left. The other—another man in a black button-down and black pants—was near her father.

Rose withdrew the silver-bladed machete, the undead in front of her immediately crouching into a pouncing position, fingers already jutting out claws while their faces changed into bony skulls with mouths filled with fangs.

"Follow your lead?" she asked her dad.

"Had hoped to take them head on, but, yes, get behind me."

She did. Her father lunged out to the right. Rose kept in line with his footsteps and kept enough distance so he wouldn't trip over her. The vampire in the black button-down jumped over them both, and landed behind her. She spun around and swiped her blade through the air, aiming to cut off the creature's head. The vampire tipped its body back—almost a perfect ninety degrees—the machete slicing through the air just above its chest. The other vampire in the turtleneck dove into the air and landed with its feet on Marcus's shoulders. Her father went down with the weight. Rose pulled a stake out of her belt and was just about to hurl it at the vampire wrestling with her father when the other one gave her a shove and sent her sidestepping several feet away. Her feet tangled and she fell to the ground, dropping both the blade and the stake.

"Oh so pretty, oh so kind. Oh so slender, please be mine," the turtlenecked vampire said as it approached her.

Rose kicked it in the shins, sending it back a step; she got to her feet. She reached for the machete on the ground, but before her fingers could grip its handle, the undead swiped its claws at her. She yanked her hand back. Quickly, she spun and kicked the creature in the gut, getting herself in between it and her blade. It was enough for her to pick up the machete and turn around and plunge it into the vampire's chest.

Please be the heart, please be the heart. Her thoughts went in time with the rapid beating of her own.

The vampire smiled. Somewhere behind her Marcus grunted. Instinct took over and she glanced over her shoulder to make sure he was okay, instead of obeying the rule to not be distracted and keep focused on the task at hand. The distraction was enough for the impaled vampire to grab her by the neck and draw her inwards.

With a yelp, limbs shaking, Rose fumbled for a stake on her belt. Hands and forearms weak, she barely held onto it just as the vampire licked her neck. With a quick jerk of her body, she pulled away and slammed the stake home beside the machete.

This time she must have struck the heart because the vampire's eyes went wide, then its skeletal head began to fold inward and its features began to smooth. Suddenly, in a burst of flesh and ash, the creature disintegrated before her. Her blade and stake fell to the ground and clanged against the gravel. Rose clamped her mouth shut so as not to inhale the vampire's fleshy and ashy remains floating on the air.

"Dad!" she shouted, picked up her tools and ran toward him.

Her father kneeled on the other vampire's stomach. In one fluid motion, he brought two stakes down into it: one through its mouth and to the back of its throat, the other through the heart. The undead broke apart and burst into ash beneath him.

"Are you okay?" she asked.

"The other one," he said, jumping to his feet, arm drawn back about to hurl a silver stake.

"It's okay, Dad. I got him."

He looked at her.

"He's dead," she said. "It's over."

Marcus put his hands on her shoulders. "That's my girl."

Shaky, she put the stake away, but kept her machete at the ready. Her father kept a stake in each hand, gripping them tight.

"Took much longer than normal. Let that be a lesson. Some of the undead are more gifted in certain areas than others." She nodded. "Ready to move on?"

As if. The adrenaline pumping through her made her legs feel like rubber. Each step barely supported her weight. "Not really."

"Then you learn another lesson tonight: to keep fighting after a kill. There are more out there, and it's up to us to stop them. Every moment we delay means another moment they have to plan and execute someone's death."

She nodded. He was right. She just hoped any other vampires they encountered tonight wouldn't be the one she couldn't stop thinking about.

7

Zach sat perched high up on a thick tree branch overlooking the river walk. Rose was below with a man he recognized as her father from her mother's funeral. If she was alone, he'd fly down and talk to her, but after seeing what the two of them were capable of, he was safer up here.

He didn't know she was a slayer. She never said anything. *And why would she?* he thought. *She just found out what I've become. Rose would never bring it up. Not so soon.*

"Trust," he said quietly. "I can't trust you, can I?"

Below, Rose continued down the pathway with her father. Zach remained in the tree. *I need to discover where your loyalties lie. For all I know now, you could simply be trying to get to me, to make me trust you.*

"It's not fair," he whispered. "Not after starting to get to know you again."

Zach stood on the tree limb and stretched his hands out to the sky. He took off from the branch and climbed higher and higher into the air before leveling off and flying above Rose and her dad.

From beside him, "Nice night, isn't it?" It was Cassie.

"How did you—"

"I'm good at being quiet."

"You'll have to teach me that trick."

"Interestingly, you already know it. You just need to tap into it and use it."

"Yeah?"

"Yeah." She ran her fingers through her black hair

and set her bangs behind her ears. The wind blowing against her messed her hair up again right afterward. "Dang it!"

"Relax."

"Whatever." She looked below. "When are you going to make your move?"

"I already fed tonight."

"So?"

"So why not have more?" She gave him a careless smile.

"I'm not in the mood."

"Wait" —she took hold of his arm, slowed him down, and made him float upright in the air beside her— "'not in the mood'? Are you feeling okay? I know your memory's out of whack right now, but not in the mood? C'mon, give me a break."

"What break? You know we don't have to feed constantly. I'm good. Had my fill."

"Yeah, but it's fun! You can swoop down, tear a head from a body and nobody can stop you. You can totally indulge yourself in your desires and get away with it. Don't you love that?"

He had to be careful what he said *and* thought. He still didn't know how to tell—if he ever could—when another vampire was probing his mind. "I'm not used to this. Not entirely. And Mother is always preaching caution."

"You worry too much. You need to let your instinct take over. That way, you'll learn faster and adjust more quickly." She glanced down below. "What say you and I head down there and surprise those two?"

No!

"What do you mean, 'no'?" she asked. She squinted her eyes and studied him.

Zach cleared his mind.

Cassie eyed him intently, trying to read his thoughts.

"Cut it out!" he said.

"Want me to tell Mother?"

"Are you five years old?"

"Telling Mother isn't childlike. Not in this case. You're hiding something from me."

"Just leave me alone, Cassie. I need some space."

She rolled her eyes. "Fine, but I'm going down there to get those two."

"Don't!"

"Why?"

"Because—I don't know. Just get a bad feeling—because they're slayers."

Cassie's eyes went wide.

"That's right. I already noticed it before you came. That's why. I thought I could protect you by not saying anything." He could tell she was debating going down there anyway. "Think about it, Cassie. There's two of them and just one of you."

"But if we both go down—"

"I told you, I already fed."

"You don't need to drink their blood, just kill them. That's two less slayers out there trying to exterminate us."

"I don't want to fight."

"As if. Guys always want to fight."

"Not me. Not right now."

She glanced down there again.

"Tell you what," he said. "Let's find someone else for you. I'll even hold them while you drink."

She pursed her lips to one side as she considered the offer. "Only if you have some with me."

Fine.

Before he could speak, she said, "Then it's settled."

She took him by the hand and they flew to the left. "That McDonald's down there is open twenty-four-seven. We're bound to find a juicy one hanging around there."

ROSE SLOWLY STEPPED out of the SUV onto the rear parking pad of the Valor address. When her feet touched the ground, the soles of her boots squished against the pavement as the blood running down her body pooled around her feet.

"You know where the washing station is," Marcus said as he rounded the front of the vehicle to the passenger side. "Next time, try not to get so much on you." He reached passed her and pulled out the blue tarp covering the seat so no blood would get on it.

"Sorry," she said. She absentmindedly scratched an itch on her forehead, in turn coating her skin with the vampire blood still on her fingers. The inky-red liquid stunk like filthy wet rags—the smell of the dead. "Gross."

"Get inside. I'll tidy up out here."

"Okay." She went to the house, a mixed feeling of pride and shame swelling in her heart. For a first night out, she didn't do too bad. All told, she came home with four kills, the last one a vampire that burst into a spray of blood before disintegrating. When asking her father for an explanation as to why that one perished differently, his answer was simply, "The turning affects everyone differently and the occasional change results in a non-standard undead mutation. There are no hard and fast rules about this. I hope I've at least taught you that much."

Yet those people were alive once, she thought. *They had friends, family, maybe even kids. Who chose for them to become what they were? It really wasn't their fault, yet I had to kill them for it.*

She went inside, wiped her feet on the mat by the door, then headed into the basement where the equipment was. A showering station was set off in a separate room right beside the main basement entrance. She went in and began peeling off her armor. Each piece was wet and slippery and in need of sterilization. Once naked, she sat on the wood-slatted bench suspended on the tiled wall and caught her breath.

I'm out of shape, she thought. *Should've spent more time on cardio or something. Combat training can only go so far endurance-wise.*

She didn't know what time it was, but guessed it was sometime after four in the morning. If she was lucky, she'd have enough time to catch about four hours sleep before school. The thought of such didn't terrify her as much as it did when her father first introduced her to her new sleep schedule: four hours in the early morning; get up, go to school; come home; eat; sleep; eat again, then prep for the night's hunt. Eventually she got used to it and was more upset at the *thought* of it than actually doing it.

Rose stood, crossed to the shower nozzle across from her, then ran the water. Its warm rain soothed her aching muscles, and with each passing moment, the blood washing away, it was like her life was being restored to her.

By the time she was done, there was a sense of removal from the night's events.

She came out of the showering room wrapped in a brown housecoat. Marcus was wiping the blades with a cloth and placing them back in their proper places on the walls.

"Good night, Dad," she said.

He didn't look back at her. "Night, hon. Sleep well. See you tomorrow."

"You, too." Rose ascended the stairs and made her way to her room. She lay on the bed and watched the stucco on the ceiling change shape in the moonlight coming in through the window. What she wouldn't give to sleep in her *own* bed tonight, instead of this place that felt more like a military bunker than an actual home.

But you're a soldier now, she thought. *Standard comforts are no longer an option.* It was going to take some getting used to. She just hoped that it would happen quickly.

◆ ◆ ◆

On the roof, Zach sat on his haunches, overlooking the backyard where he'd watched Rose and her father enter the house from the shadows.

So this is where they hide, he thought. Getting here was easy, and he was surprised no other vampire had attempted to find this stronghold before. *Or, at least, find it and live to tell about it.*

After him and Cassie finished feeding off a chubby white guy with a bad haircut behind the McDonald's, they flew in circles around each other to celebrate before parting ways.

"Just be sure to get back soon," Cassie had said. "It's going to be dawn soon. Usually just after five."

"Okay." He'd keep a careful watch on the horizon.

Now, on the roof of the slayers' home, Zach debated whether he should break in and talk to Rose, or just simply let it go for the time being and head back to the crypt.

He stood, walked up the shingles to the middle of the

house, then went back down the other side. A glimmer of white sparkled in his peripheral. He looked. Fastened to the chimney was a camera.

"Uh oh," he said, and immediately jumped up into the sky.

♦ ♦ ♦

"Our boy is out there alone?" Mira asked.

"Yes, but hasn't been for long," Cassie said.

The two stood beside Cassie's coffin in the crypt.

"The sun will rise very soon. If he is not back in time, he will burn."

"He also needs to learn to budget his time better." The remark was met with a sharp slap to the cheek.

"Zach is still learning, my dear, or did you forget?"

Cassie hung her head. "No, Mother. I'm sorry."

Mira crossed her arms. "I don't want to see you right now." And walked past her.

Rain had just lay in his coffin and already had his eyes closed. "Does she know where he is?" he asked.

"No."

"What if he doesn't return?"

"Then we start again."

"I see."

She leaned in and gave her husband a soft kiss on the mouth. "But he will return, my love. He now has reason to be careful."

A loud screech filled the chamber as, above, the door to the crypt opened.

"See?" Mira said.

The door screeched again as it was closed. Zach came down the steps.

"Mother, Father," he said. "Cassie." She stuck her

hand up out of her coffin and gave him a wave. "Where's Wil?"

"Sleeping already," Mira said. "You are late."

"I know. I'm sorry."

"I was worried."

"You were?"

She held out a hand and glided along the floor to him. "Oh my son, I always worry about my children. I did not want to see you fall captive by the dawn."

He touched her hand on his cheek. "Thank you, but I'm fine."

Mira smiled, slowly slid her hand off his face, then floated to her coffin in the middle of the room. Zach retired to his own.

With the taste of blood still on his tongue, he lay in his coffin and closed the wooden lids. Mira telekinetically lifted the stone lid and sealed him in. A moment later, he heard her do the same to her own coffin. Here, in the darkness, safe and tucked away from the world and even the *underworld* of the crypt, he let his thoughts drain from his mind in the hopes of quickly drifting off to sleep.

Eyes closed, nothing but blackness for his sight, he heard a voice in his head: *Show me what you saw tonight.* The voice sounded like his mother's, but slightly different. A red shadow with a female silhouette faded into view along the matte of darkness before him. It wore a dress and had long, flowing hair. *I can see the sky, the stars. Cassie.*

"Mother . . ." Zach whispered.

The next words came more as an *impression* rather than a coherent statement. *Relax. Son. Sleep.*

The red figure floated closer toward him until she took up nearly all of his mind's eye.

"Let's see . . ." he said. Zach focused on it and willed it to move from view until he saw only darkness again.

Relax. Son—

He pushed the figure aside once more when she began to surface into view again.

Rel—

Darkness. *Keep focused,* he thought. *No one else. Just me, the dark, the quiet.* No more words from his mother in the coffin not far from him. Zach realized what he'd done.

He blocked his thoughts from her.

9

THE NEXT MORNING, Rose got ready in her room, and headed to the kitchen for a bite to eat before facing the day. When she came into the kitchen, her father stood facing the counter, mug of coffee in his hand, just staring at the granite countertop.

Rose got out a bowl, a spoon from the drawer, milk from the fridge and cereal from the cupboard. Ever since her mom died, her father stopped laying out breakfast for her. Perhaps doing so was too painful a reminder of how things used to be.

"Morning," she said as she prepared her breakfast.

Marcus took a sip of his coffee, his eyes never leaving the countertop.

Oooh-kay, she thought, poured the milk and put the jug back in the fridge. She took her cereal to the table and started eating.

"You okay, Dad?" she asked after her third mouthful.

He merely sighed, took another sip of coffee, then slowly turned around.

"What?" she asked.

He cleared his throat, and didn't make eye contact when he spoke. "I checked over last night's surveillance tapes."

Rose glanced away. The cameras were reverse-thermal imaging cameras specially made for slayer households. They displayed cool objects against warmer ones. "A precaution," her dad had said. "Bloodsuckers don't show up on conventional film, so we use these and can see their cool bodies against the warmer air."

In the kitchen, her dad continued, "Rose, look at me."

"What?"

"There was someone on the roof."

Her heart leapt into her throat and she gagged on her cereal. She pulled a sheet of paper towel from the roll standing in the middle of the table and wiped the milk from her mouth. "Really?"

He nodded.

"A prowler or . . . one of them?"

"One of them." He took a breath. "A prowler wouldn't be on the roof."

"Right. Stupid question."

"The strange thing was" —he pulled away from the counter and took a step closer to the table— "it was a vampire we've seen before. Well, someone we've seen before."

Uh oh. Not—

"It was Zach," he said, his face solemn. "You said he'd gone missing, and now we know where he's gone."

Act surprised. She cleared her throat. "Really? You mean, he was . . . um . . . turned?" She couldn't help but let a small smile crack her lips.

"What?"

"Nothing. I'm just really glad he's okay."

"He's not okay, Rose. He's . . . dead."

Despite it being something she already knew, it pained her heart to think of him that way.

"I'm sorry," he said, and set his mug down on the table.

Tears welled in her eyes. It wasn't an act. "Me, too."

A heavy silence sunk in between them. It was her father who broke it. When he spoke, Rose could tell he was trying his best to be sensitive. "I think he followed us here. He was probably out last night and saw us. Whether he understood *why* we were out, I don't know, but if he recognized you from things . . . before . . . then it makes sense he'd come after you."

"I don't think he 'came after me.'"

"Sorry. Wrong words. I meant followed you, you know, as a way to connect with the life he had before."

Though she already knew the answer, she wanted to see how much he knew. "Do you think he . . . remembers?"

"Probably. Most of them do. I've heard them talk over the years. I've heard them mention places they used to go and people they used to see."

"I wonder if he remembers me? Remembers us?"

Marcus sighed. "I don't know. I can only imagine how hard this is for you to hear. That's the danger of this job: you risk losing someone you lo—someone you care about to them." He picked up his coffee and took a sip. "I know, because I lost someone to them, too." His eyes met hers. "We both did."

She thought about it for a moment. Should she mention she'd already talked to Zach? Should she say that, yes, the connection they once shared was still present?

I just don't want to say anything that would get him in trouble. He seemed so different when I talked to him. Different than the other . . . undead . . . we've fought. I just don't know what to make of this. "What should I do?"

He gazed past her. "Protocol states to live your life as usual, to not let on to any undead spies or those working for them that you know something. That's all we can do right now." He planted both palms on the table and leaned toward her. His eyes turned to ice. "But promise me this: if Zach tries to contact you, you get away from him as safely as you can. Run or fight, whatever it takes—preferably run—but you get away and you tell me. Am I clear?"

His tone pierced her to the core. It was the same tone he used when she got in trouble. Heart beating hard, all she managed was a weak, "Yes."

He kept his eyes on hers. "I'm serious, Rose. This is life or death, and I will not take chances with my daughter's life. I will not lose you like I lost your mother."

She put her face in her hands and began to sob. Despite her feelings for Zach, it was his kind that killed her mother. All she could do was cry.

From behind her hands, she heard her father pull away from the table. "I have an appointment with a client. You will go to school then come straight home. Take your cell. I'll have mine. Notice anything suspicious—no matter how seemingly ordinary—if you think something is out of place or if someone is watching you, you call me right away. Understood?"

She nodded.

Marcus rounded to her side of the table and put his arms around her. He gently rocked her back and forth in her seat. "It'll be okay, baby girl. It'll be okay." He held her a few moments more then kissed the top of her head.

Rose pulled away from her hands and used the crumpled-up paper towel to wipe her nose and eyes. "I love you, Dad."

"Love you, too, pumpkin." He smiled, then left the kitchen. "Come straight here after school. No exceptions."

She nodded.

Sitting there, stomach and heart in a knot, she didn't feel much like eating, but her new lifestyle demanded she had breakfast whether she wanted to or not. She stirred the cereal around in her bowl. It was soggy.

10

THE LIGHTS OF Rose's family room were dim, the big brown couch in front of the TV soft and cozy. The house was quiet, and Zach and Rose were alone. He sat on the couch, one leg folded under the other, watching her as she sifted through the DVDs in the shelving unit that held the TV.

"I've seen all these a thousand times," she said, going over the spines of the cases.

"Yeah, but I haven't," he replied.

She stood back from the unit and put her hands on her hips. Even from behind, she was beautiful, her long brown hair the kind that made his fingers ache with the desire to run them through it.

"I don't know, what are you in the mood for?" she asked.

"Wouldn't mind something funny."

"Don't got much of that. Mom likes dramas and mysteries, so she's overloaded us with those. Dad's not much into movies other than old James Dean flicks. Hmmm . . ." She scanned the shelves then pulled out a movie. "*Billy Madison?*"

Zach chuckled. "I think the last time I saw that was way back on a rerun."

She pulled out another. "*Ace Ventura?*"

"Nothing current, huh?"

Rose looked at the DVDs in her hands. "No." With a sigh, she brought them over to him and sat beside him on the couch. She held them in each hand as if weighing them. "Wish there was more, but this is about it."

"Think your folks will mind if they come home and I'm here?"

She didn't take her eyes off the movies. "Probably not. Their main thing is no boys in my bedroom, and if they are, the door stays open, yada, yada, yada."

"My folks are the same." With a smirk, he added, "With your parents out, this whole house is kind of like your bedroom, huh?"

She looked at him with those lovely hazel eyes of hers. "You're such a guy."

"That's not what I meant."

"Oh yeah?" She set the DVDs down behind her then scooched over so she was right up next to him. "What did you mean?"

The words wouldn't form. Man, did he love this girl. Because they were so young, he just prayed it would last. He knew it would on his end, but with still a couple years to go before graduation never mind what came after that, he hoped she wouldn't grow tired of him and one day they'd be together forever. "I love you."

She pouted her lips and blushed. "I love you, too."

"No, I mean I *really* love you. I love you so much."

She placed her hand on his cheek, her touch soothing and warm. Zach put his hand against hers, electricity running through his body.

"I really love you, too. This has really rocked my world," she said.

"Mine, too."

Their gaze lingered on the others', then Zach leaned forward and kissed her. At first their mouths merely brushed against each other's, but soon they were pressing together, hard and true. Their tongues licked, slid together, and with each rhythmic movement of their lips,

Zach poured himself into her, hoping each expression of affection told her how much she meant to him.

He drew her in closer and wrapped his arms around her, pulling her body against his, unable to get enough of her. He so desperately wanted to pull her inside himself, share her body and become one with her.

Rose returned his caress and took his face in her hands, kissing him all the harder, her touch, love and embrace becoming his whole world.

Rose, my sweet Rose. I love you. Forever and always. "I love you," he whispered. Her lips left his and didn't return. Zach opened his eyes and found himself in the dark, the plush lining of the coffin wrapped around him like a cocoon.

"I love you," he whispered. "Forever and always."

◆ ◆ ◆

If there was any one class that was Rose's least favorite, it was Math. More specifically, it was this new curriculum the school division had the grade on. Rumor had it everybody was flunking, so she wasn't alone in that department. Every scrawl of chalk at the front of the room was just a hodge podge of numbers, letters and lines.

This sucks, she thought, one hand under her chin, the other holding a pen and copying down what was on the blackboard. *What* she was copying, she hadn't a clue. She'd figure it out later if she remembered to review her notes. Mrs. Matuzak droned on and on at the front of the room, trying to convey the Greek that was on the board.

Math was the last thing on Rose's mind right now. After what her father told her this morning, she felt stuck. Just simply doing what her dad said would keep things nice and easy, but if Zach's presence on their roof was an indicator, then he probably wanted to see her.

Except he can't be out in the sun, she thought. She looked out the window. *And it's sunny today.*

The thought of going to the cemetery after school made her heart beat rapidly with anticipation, but with the sun out, she wouldn't see Zach anyway. She didn't even know where he hung out at Eagle Park or if he even lived there.

She could go and visit her mom's grave. Surely her dad couldn't get mad at her for that.

And I really should go and see her. She sighed. *I miss you, Mom. Lots. Feels like since you've been gone, everything's changed. It's hard to even remember how things used to be. Wish I could go back.* Rose compared her notes to what was on the board. She had missed a line and now had to squeeze in a handful of numbers in between a stack of others. *This sucks.*

The rest of the day moved slower than molasses, and when the three o'clock bell rang, she was more than happy to get out of there. She hit her locker, packed her bag, and threw it over her shoulder. Every step from the school to the bus stop was riddled with the question of whether she should go home or go to the cemetery.

Her heart ached at the real reason for going, though. *You just want to see Zach and you're using Mom as an excuse.* She shook her head. *I'm sorry, Mom.*

At the bus stop, she checked her watch. It was 3:12. *Dad's usually done around five-ish and, depending where he is, could be home right after.* The bus was just up the street. *I could keep it brief and see Mom. Zach won't be there anyway. Still sunny.* She waited, glancing around, hoping for a distraction. Nothing but kids her age milling about, some walking home, others gathering around the bus stop.

When the bus pulled up, she got on, paid her fare, and found a seat next to the window.

"I hate this," she muttered. Indecisiveness was something that always got under her skin, and bothered her even more so when *she* was the one being indecisive.

When the rest of the kids piled on, the bus headed down the street. It would pass by the cemetery on the way downtown, where she would transfer and take another bus to the Slayer House.

She checked her watch. 3:18. She quickly ran a timetable through her head, averaging bus and wait times. *It's going to be close.*

Ten minutes later, the iron-gated entrance to Eagle Park Cemetery came into view. Anxiety snuck in and Rose closed her eyes. *Just tell Dad you had to visit Mom. See what he says.*

Checking out the window for the next stop, she took a deep breath, and pulled the stop cord.

II

Marcus wrapped up a meeting with the last clients of the day, an elderly couple looking to downsize after being empty-nesters for several years. Once back in his vehicle, he checked his watch. It was just after 3:30. He reviewed his appointment book.

Should do a quick follow up for the morning meeting and verify a place to get together. Why some people wait for the last possible second is beyond me. He dialed the number to a young couple that were planning on buying their first home and finally settled on meeting them at Tim Horton's, then dialed the Slayer House to make sure Rose was there. No answer, not even after eight rings.

"Your bus better be late," he said, and put his business cell phone on the passenger seat.

He pulled into traffic and headed toward the Valor house.

◆ ◆ ◆

"I really don't know what to do, Mom," Rose said, standing in front of her mother's grave. "Wish you were here to talk Dad down. Not that he's being unreasonable, mind you, it's just that you were always good at calming the waters when things got rough between us."

A brief mental flash of her mother's ashes actually comprehending what she said crossed her mind's eye.

"What would you do?" she asked. "What if—and just hear me out—what if Dad was a vampire and you were still a slayer? Would you go after him and hunt him down? Even kill him? Did you guys ever talk about this?" A gust of warm wind blew across her face. "I'd almost pose the question to Dad, but ever since you . . . died . . . he seems more dedicated to eradicating the undead than ever. Hmph. What do I know? Never mind. He could have always been like this and I just never saw it. I only found out about this side of you guys after you passed away." *Did it hurt, Mom? Did you feel them bite you?* She sniffled. "I hate to say it, but a part of me wishes they had turned you into one of them instead. Maybe I'd still get to see you somehow. Maybe even though you were one of them, you'd remember me, Dad, the life we all had before."

She fell to her knees. "I so badly just want to cling to the past, to hang onto the old way. I'm only sixteen so I know I don't know a whole lot about life, but I'm not stupid either. Naïve, sure, but not stupid. I know that kids shouldn't have to grow up overnight. I know it's not fair that I have to suddenly take your place and continue the family tradition." Tears welled up in her eyes. "I'm not ready for it yet, Mom. Not ready at all. Physically, sure, I'm working on it. Dad's trained me enough to stand on my own against the undead, but inside, where it counts . . . . How did you do it? How did you write your life off for someone you loved?"

I still love Zach. No matter what he's become. He doesn't remember me the same way he used to, but he doesn't not *remember me either.* "Can you read my mind? Can the dead know what I'm thinking or feeling? Can you even hear me?" She didn't know what she was saying, but it felt so good to let it out, to speak whatever she thought.

"It's sunny out, Mom. Zach can't come out in the sun. I want to see him and I know he's here. My heart's beating quickly just thinking about it. I know what he is, but is it wrong to just talk to him, to spend time with him if nothing bad happens?"

Rose wiped her eyes. "I wish you'd reply. I really don't know what to do right now."

◆ ◆ ◆

Marcus was almost at the Slayer House when the sinking feeling Rose wouldn't be there settled firmly in his stomach. He pulled over and dialed the house again. Same thing: multiple rings, no answer.

He closed his eyes and let his disappointment wash over him. "Oh, Rose."

He set the car in gear and headed to the one place he knew she'd be: Eagle Park Cemetery.

Marcus just hoped he was wrong.

◆ ◆ ◆

Rose was back on her feet, staring at the engraving of her mother's name on the columbarium, every so often glancing past it to the rest of the cemetery beyond for anyone who might also be among the graves.

Her loyalty was to her father, she knew, but her heart belonged to Zach. That much was clear. If it wasn't, she wouldn't be having doubts about continuing as a slayer, about disobeying her father, and if coming here had been the right choice or not.

"I miss you, Zach," she whispered. To her mother: "I'm sorry. I wish I was older. This would be so much easier. I could just leave home, go my own way, and get done what I need to do." She sniffled again. "You'll still love me, won't you? Even if I choose Zach over Dad?"

Her mother's grave was silent. Not that she expected a reply, but it would have been nice had there been some internal switch set off, one where she felt a rush of peace or an assurance everything was going to be okay in the end.

The minutes ticked by.

Rose glanced around the gravestones again.

She saw her father coming in her direction.

A hollow smack struck her in the chest; the look on his face said he was pissed. *I am so dead.* He was still near the cemetery gate so she didn't know if he saw her or not. Legs rubbery, she made a break for it and took off in the opposite direction, running in between the grave markers, up other aisles of the dead, in between other gravestones.

"Rose!" her father shouted behind her. "Get back here! I see you!"

"Ohcrapohcrapohcrapohcrap." *I'm so dead, so dead. WhatdoIdowhatdoIdowhatdoIdo?* Heart racing, she ran further into the cemetery. She peeked over her shoulder; her father was running as well.

He's a hunter. He'll find me. I'm so stupid, stupid, stupid.

"Rose! Now!" He was using *The Tone,* the one that was low and carried a hard edge that spoke to her conscience and said he meant business.

The smart choice would be to just give up and face him, get yelled at and disciplined. But there was more at stake. This was also about Zach. *All* about Zach.

"Rose!"

He was getting close.

Rose ran, hopped over a gravestone, ran across another aisle, and jumped over another stone. Somewhere in the back of her mind she felt guilty for trampling on the grounds of the deceased, the areas where just six feet below the bodies were buried. She even said "Sorry" once or twice as she did her best to weave around trees and mausoleums.

Eventually you're going to run out of places to hide. I know! Somehow get out of here, hop on a bus and get home. Then when he comes, you can say you've been there all along! Yeah! "He's already seen you." *Crap!*

She took a sharp left, sprinted, then hid behind a wide oak tree. She peered around it and couldn't see her dad.

Heat rose up against the back of her neck and arms. From behind, a set of hands attached to clothed arms on fire grabbed her and her feet left the ground, soaring up a couple stories before landing. A door closed in front of her. The hot hands released her clothes. She spun around to see the orange glow of a young man frantically patting out the flames covering his upper body before it all went dark.

Rose?" Zach barely got her name out before clasping a hand around his neck. He coughed, the skin and muscles of his neck already swollen from being on fire.

"I can't see," she said. "Zach?"

"It's" —he coughed again; it felt like he was regurgitating a fistful of razorblades— "it's me." When he swallowed, it was like swallowing a small sea urchin.

"Are you okay?"

"I'll live."

"Where are you?"

He glanced up in the direction of her voice, his keen night vision showing her groping at the dark. Slowly, the skin covering his hand and arm screaming, he reached up and touched her fingers.

She snapped her hand back. "Ow. You're burning hot!"

"I'll cool down," he said and sat on the floor. He had to wait a moment for his throat to settle before speaking. "We need to keep quiet. There are . . . there are others in here beyond this room."

His sharp hearing picked up her breath catching in her throat. "You mean—?"

"My family."

Rose proceeded cautiously in the dark, her slow steps allowing him enough time to put a hand on her leg to stop her before she'd step on him.

"I'm here," he said. "Sit down. There's a small wall beside you."

She reached out, located the wall, then carefully sat down. She didn't say anything.

"Why so quiet?" he asked.

"I was tol—I heard of you, you know, vampires, catching fire in the daylight. Just never thought I'd see it."

"It's not the first time it's happened."

"No?"

"No. When I first . . . awoke . . . I went outside and started burning up pretty quick."

"Does it hurt?"

"Yes."

"I'm so sorry."

"Don't be. I acted without thinking. I'll be all right. I'll heal."

She felt around in the dark, found his shoulder, and set a hand upon it. She pulled her hand back when the hot, burnt fabric of his jacket crumbled beneath her touch. "Is that you?"

"No. Just the jacket."

She sighed relief. "You won't die?"

Right now the pain was so intense he wished he would. "No. The fire needs to penetrate to my heart. There wasn't enough time for that to happen, thank goodness. I'll be fine by nightfall."

"So quick?"

"If it was any other kind of wound, it'd be quicker. Fire takes longer."

The sound of her sniffling back tears pained him in a way the fire never could. *This shouldn't bother me. Not her feelings. I* don't *have feelings.* He let the next wave of searing pain overtake him, rode its current, then welcomed the subtle relief that followed. *Except for her, it seems. She gets to me. Rose. I know who you are. What we were.*

"Why were you running?" he asked.

She exhaled slowly, the undercurrent of quivering breath enough to tell him he had touched on a tender point. "My dad," she said softly.

"You're not in trouble, are you?"

"Not like that. But, yeah, I *will* be in trouble when I get home. I—" She didn't finish.

Zach squeezed his hands into fists, stretching the burnt skin, then slowly released them. "It's okay. You can tell me."

"I don't think you'd understand."

You'd be surprised. I already know, Rose, I already know, which is why I didn't call you on saying you heard vampires catch on fire in the daylight. "Are you sure?"

"Yeah. For now, anyway, but thanks for asking."

The door at the top of the stairs leading down into the crypt was partly open and Zach could sense Rose's unease.

I could look inside her mind, get the information I need. The strong pull to do so was almost as overwhelming as the darkness that crept in when he had to feed, the power of reading another's thoughts so strong and so appealing it was difficult to suppress. He understood right then why his mother exercised this ability so readily. He just couldn't bring himself to violate Rose like that. At least when it came to divulging something she wouldn't willingly share.

"Are you scared?" he asked.

"Not really. Just upset with myself."

"Don't be."

"You don't get it."

"I don't need to. I'm a vampire, remember? I know what it's like to do . . . questionable . . . things. I know what it's like to regret my actions but at the same time be unsure if indeed it was the wrong thing to do."

She released an airy chuckle. "Are you reading my mind now?" He heard her snap her mouth shut.

You shouldn't have said that. He pretended he didn't hear the questions. "Hm?"

"Nothing. But you're right. I know what it's like to feel that way, too."

The rough scraping sound of stone sliding on stone came from the dark below.

"What's that?" she whispered.

A smooth, soft female voice rose from the crypt. "Zach? Why are you up there?" It was Mira.

Now I have to talk to her in front of Rose. He didn't mean it as a bad thing, but he had hoped he'd let Rose out of the mausoleum before anyone below awoke. "I am finished sleeping, Mother. I thought I'd come up here so as to not disturb you or the others." Rose's quickening heartbeat sounded in his right ear. To Rose, he whispered: "You need to go."

They got up and Zach led her to the door. He'd explain his burnt appearance to his mother after. Just as he was about to open the mausoleum door, Mira spoke from behind them: "Who's this?"

Rose's heart rate sped up even more.

Zach focused and said inside her mind: *It's okay. You are safe. I won't let anything happen to you.*

He heard her heartbeat slow, but only a little.

"Mother," he said, "this is . . . a friend. Someone who I haven't seen in a *long* time."

"I see," Mira said. "And she is here because?"

Suddenly Rose blurted, "I won't tell anyone, I swear. I'm sorry. Zach brought me here. I didn't know . . . didn't think there'd be . . . I—I can't see you. Is there a light?"

"Rose," Zach said firmly. To Mira: "She is someone I used to know. She didn't know you were here."

"Nor, it seemed, did she know we were *all* here, but you already said too much in that regard, Zach. What did we talk about?"

No outsiders allowed in the crypt. It was one of the first things you taught me.

She answered him telepathically. *Then what is she doing here? If your father found out, he'd confine you to your coffin until you were so weak from not feeding you wouldn't be able to fend for yourself. Then he'd set you on a group of slayers.*

Please don't tell him, he told her. *I'll show her out.*

It's daylight!

Zach said, "I know. I was already outside."

Rose gave him a quizzical stare. She obviously had no idea what he was talking about.

"I know, son. I can see your skin." Mira gracefully held out her hand. "Come, let us go down and I will tend to you. As for your friend" —she looked to Rose— "she can join us."

13

Marcus searched the cemetery, running in between the aisles of graves, passing around mausoleums, doubling back and walking the main road that snaked through Eagle Park.

Rose was nowhere to be found.

If she thinks she could sneak off and, I don't know, head home and pretend like nothing happened, boy, is she in for a surprise. He ran his hands through his hair, the roots damp with sweat, and stopped his stride back toward the car. Glancing over his shoulder and staring at the gravestones beyond, he sensed that Rose hadn't snuck off but instead was still here somewhere. *The undead live here, hiding inside the tombs.* "Rose, if you came here for Zach, there will be hell to pay."

He couldn't shake the feeling he was being watched, yet he also usually had that feeling, years of expecting the worse and always being on guard having filed his nerves to razor sensitivity. Part of it was simple paranoia; the other experience.

As he walked to the SUV, Marcus came up with a plan.

◆ ◆ ◆

This isn't the family I know, Rose thought. The dark of the crypt projected a chill that seeped through her pores and tickled her bones. The woman, Zach's so-called mother, led them to the main floor of the underground tomb.

Rose tugged on Zach's sleeve. "I can't see much," she whispered.

"You're not supposed to," he said.

"I'll fix that," his mother said, and in a flash of light from a match, she lit a torch on the far wall, above a coffin.

The stench of rot and earth filled Rose's nostrils, as if lighting the torch had suddenly set off her sense of smell. A stone, ornately-carved coffin sat in the middle of the cold floor; others lined each side of the room in their own cubbies in the mud-caked stone walls.

"Welcome to our home, Rose," Zach's mother said, her gaze suggesting that even though he hadn't properly introduced her, the fact that she knew her name after probing her mind suddenly placed her in a position of authority.

Rose understood that because here she was outnumbered a seeming four to one, five including Zach.

"Mother," Zach said as if catching on to the woman's game. "Let's start over. Mother, this is Rose. Rose, this is my mother, Mira."

Rose eyed the woman in the flowing black dress. She leaned close to Zach and whispered: "Your *real* mom? What about—"

"Barbara Mohansen?" Mira said.

Rose nodded.

"She took care of Zach while his father and I waited to bring him home. It's all a little complicated, my dear, but rest assured we love Zach because he is our own."

"I see." *I'll let him explain it to me instead.*

Zach shifted on his feet; uncomfortable.

The grinding of stone on stone pierced Rose's ears and set her on edge. A pair of wooden casket doors squeaked open and a girl with a taut black ponytail wearing a plaid-skirted schoolgirl's uniform sat up in one of the coffins and said, "Smells lovely. You brought one home" —she glanced around— "Mother?" She jumped out of the coffin and landed beside Rose. Suddenly the schoolgirl's visage transformed from one of pale skin and smooth features to a skeletal hag with a large mouth and sharp teeth.

Mira clapped her hands together. "CASSANDRA!"

The schoolgirl growled and grabbed Rose by the shoulders. Rose yelped. Swiftly, Zach was in between them and shoved the girl back.

"She's not for feeding on," Mira said, her voice as cold as ice.

The schoolgirl with the rotted, skeletal face looked at Mira, her inky black eyes conveying confusion.

"She is not for feeding," Mira said again.

The schoolgirl hissed at Rose before her jagged and bony features melted away, revealing a young girl again.

"I'm sorry," Zach said to Rose. He put his arm around her to help her stop shaking.

"I'm scared," she whispered, though it was only partly true. It was more the weirdness of all this that put her off than the actual fear of the undead.

"Rose, this is my sister, Cassie." To Cassie: "And she's sorry."

Cassie looked at him, looked at Mira, then at Rose. She cast her eyes to the ground and folded her hands in front of her hips. "Yes. I'm sorry. I didn't know you knew Zach." She arced an eyebrow at Mira, as if asking if she said the right thing. Mira nodded.

"Can we go?" Rose asked him.

"I can't. Not until dark. You don't need to be afraid. I'm here, and they won't hurt you."

More stone slid across stone and wooden lids

squeaked on rusty hinges as a large male vampire sat up in his coffin. He looked at Rose, then at Mira. "I see," was all he said, then lay back down and let the wooden lids close and the stone one slide back over him.

Cassie snickered. "You're in big trouble."

"Am not," Zach said.

"Are to."

"Am not."

"Are to."

Rose just glanced up at the crypt's ceiling and waited the bickering out.

"Kids!" Mira said.

Stone slid upon stone again and Rose thought the big vampire was going to jump out and set them all straight. Instead, the stone lid of another coffin moved, hinges creaked as a set of wooden lids slowly opened, and a young man sat up.

"Rose, this is Wil, my brother," Zach said.

Wil eyed Rose up and down, then raised his eyebrows and slowly nodded. "Hellooo, gorgeous."

She blushed without meaning to.

"Shut it, Wil," Zach said.

"Sure. Whatever you say," he said, all the while maintaining eye contact with Rose.

"Anyway," Zach said to her, "I won't force you to stay, and if you're scared, I understand." He took his hands in hers. Their coolness sent a shiver up her arms. "But I'd be honored if you remained until nightfall."

His voice filled her head. *Don't worry. I'm here. You have nothing to be afraid of.*

Taking a deep breath, she said, "Okay." It was either that, or go home and face her father.

◆ ◆ ◆

Marcus packed the SUV and ensured he had all his equipment. Whether Rose was still in the cemetery or not, he wouldn't allow it to be a dangerous place anymore. Tonight, whatever unholiness lurked there would fall by his blade.

16

IF ZACH'S NEW family was anything, it was welcoming, something Rose hadn't expected from the undead, especially after everything her father told her about them being monsters. She knew of their fiercer side and their lust for blood, yet, it seemed, they also had the ability to control themselves when around a meal. Still, despite their non-offensive behavior—except for the incident with Cassie—Rose remained on edge, just in case.

"They can't be trusted," her father had told her early in her training. "They are wilier and more deceptive than the devil himself. Every word from their lips is poison. Should one ever speak to you, ignore them and move in for the kill."

Except her father didn't count on her meeting someone she once knew. Didn't count on a complex web of emotion, confusion, and relationships.

But he couldn't have known, she thought, so decided not to hold it against him.

Zach's family was so open to her being there and exuded such warmth toward her that fear of repercussion of disobeying her dad began to melt away.

The hours went by, and Zach's family made her the focus, dishing out question after question about the world above ground, how she knew Zach, and why she found it so easy to trust him. Oddly, Zach hardly got a word in edgewise. Every time he opened his mouth to speak, his mother would say something first and redirect the conversation to focus on Rose.

The way the vampires playfully bickered and joked with one another really brought an air of security and camaraderie to the dim confines of the crypt. They were no different than any other family in that way. The overwhelming sense of belonging swept over Rose in a powerful rush of love and affection.

Over and over words and phrases echoed throughout her soul: *Welcome. Any friend of Zach's is a friend of ours. You're safe. We won't hurt you. All is well. Forever. We care about you. Trust us. Nothing is wrong. Relax. You're home. We're family. We love you.*

She knew this feeling. It was the same as it was when she first met Zach's human family, welcomed in with open arms right from the start. The way Zach's mom had hugged her before she even had a chance to take her shoes off at the door. His dad looking at her with a fatherly nod of approval. The house smelling rich with home cooked meals, neat and tidy. The kind of place you could easily feel secure in.

Zach's new family emitted the same sense of belonging despite their dark and morbid surroundings. If anything, there was a real sense of authenticity in their interest in her and their desire to bridge the gap between human and vampire.

◆ ◆ ◆

Marcus parked the SUV one street over from the cemetery. He rounded the back of the vehicle and got himself armed. Stakes, garlic steam bombs, and a UV flashbomb were placed in their appropriate pouches and compartments on his belt and in his long black overcoat. A pair of silver-plated machetes were sheathed across his back, their hilts jutting out just above the coat's collar.

Rose hadn't come home. She hadn't answered her cell.

He prayed she was all right, and he prayed that tonight he would be granted the power to eradicate the undead from Eagle Park Cemetery. And should Rose be here, that she would be safe and learn a firm lesson about associating with the undead.

Even if that undead was the love of her life.

◆ ◆ ◆

Zach and Rose stood on top of the vampire mausoleum, their arms around each other. Being this close to her and feeling her body heat through his clothes made him long for the life he had before. Despite still not remembering all of it, it seemed that every moment spent with her was like finding keys to a series of locks, each key opening up parts of himself and awakening hidden memories.

The air was crisp, the sky clear, the moon a sliver of bright white light in the heavens. Each star stood prominent against the black night sky, their light more than just the mere pinpricks they used to be, each one producing a sphere of light as if God Himself was behind the curtain of black and sending the brightness of a floodlight from behind.

"So quiet," Rose said.

The cars passing the street some quarter kilometer away filled Zach's ears, as did the sounds of footsteps from those walking the sidewalks, the voices of those speaking loud and clear as if he was standing right next to them. "Not to me."

"You can hear everything, huh?"

"Not everything, but enough. Everything I see, taste, touch, smell and hear is amplified. Or so I was told. I don't remember what it was like before. I can only imagine, and when I do, everything feels muffled, frustrating."

"And when I speak?"

"It's like an angel is talking to me."

She giggled. "No, silly. What I meant was, when I'm this close, is it like I'm shouting?"

"No. Maybe to you it'd sound that way, but like I said, this is all I know so you sound normal."

She gave him a squeeze. He returned it in kind.

"How much of *us* do you remember?" she asked.

"I don't know. I couldn't give you a ratio or a percentage or anything. I suppose I remember enough, like who you are and some things that I guess meant a great deal to me because I can easily recall them. As for every single moment we had, no, I don't remember." He hoped she wouldn't get offended by that.

"Well, if it makes you feel any better, I don't remember every single moment either. No one can. We just remember the stuff that touches us, or impacts us, or for one reason or another means a lot." She squeezed him again. "What *do* you remember?"

He closed his eyes, reveling in her embrace. In the crypt below, he heard his father pacing. The other three were already out for the night's feeding.

Images danced before his eyes. He pulled a handful out from his mind's eye and let each unfold as if each were a present unto themselves. "I see a theatre, and some steps leading down from it. It's night, and you have your arm hooked around mine. You're wearing a gray wool sweater, blue jeans and, I think, a red shirt underneath. Your head is on my shoulder. I can't see your face, but I know your eyes are open because you're negotiating the steps just fine. I don't remember the name of the movie, but there's this sense of fatigue, as if whatever we just sat through was long. I'm sore from sitting. We cross the street to the parking lot and go to my other parents' car. I open the door for you and you get in. I don't know what the color of the car is, but the interior is dark gray. I go to my side and get in as well, and we sit there in the parking lot. Your hands are under your thighs and there's this look on your face as if you're waiting for something. I see the steering wheel in front of me, my hands dreading to touch it, because if I do, then it means it's time to go home.

"At night, I feel alive. Not just now but always. Day time was never for me. I suppose now I finally learn that that's true. In the car, I hope you don't mind just sitting there with me. You shiver, so I start the car and turn the heat on. I desperately want to hold you, keep you warm, smell your hair and kiss your cheek. I'm afraid that if I do, my heart will fall, and though I already love you, I'm scared that I'll be lost in you forever.

"As if sensing my unease, you reach over and curl my hand in yours. A moment later you bring my fingers to your lips and kiss them ever so softly. I die inside, knowing that each minute spent with you means another minute of my life is gone, lost somewhere in the world you've created for us, a kind of sphere where it's just you and me and whatever we want.

"I look at you. You look at me. My heart aches. No one leans in first. We do it together, and our lips meet."

Rose pulled slightly away from him and looked into his eyes. Hers were coated with tears and she nibbled on her lower lip.

"I don't remember what happened after that," he said. "I just remember closing my eyes and falling into you."

She drew him close, and like that night in the car, their lips found each other's and for the first time since waking to his new life, Zach felt like he had just awoken into another one.

This one made of her.

RAIN STOOD BESIDE Mira's coffin, gazing up at the crypt's roof. Zach's memory of that night by the theatre with Rose reminded him of someone he knew long ago, before Mira, during his early life as a vampire. Her name had been Gabriella, and he'd known her in the latter part of the sixteenth century. Life had been easier back then. Though they were hunted by slayers and the politics of both the vampires and the slayers were already in place throughout the land, the lack of human population made living and hiding much easier. Months would sometimes go by when neither he nor Gabriella would set sight on another undead. Even the humans they came across to feed upon were usually met four or five days apart. One time it was over two weeks between feedings, and though he and Gabriella grew weaker by the day, they grew stronger with each other.

Waking to the night sky in the forest in each other's arms, each needing to rely on the other for the strength to stand, interdependency brought them together both inside and out.

Gabriella was lost in a fire, one set by her own body when a slayer had captured her and kept her in a small hut. Rain had come for her just before dawn. Only one slayer stood guard at the hut's door, and was quickly dispatched when Rain cleaved off his head. He went in, found his sweetheart weak and bound. About to drag the guard's body into the hut for her to feed upon, dawn grew on the horizon. He quickly closed the hut's door, thinking its dark embrace would be enough to protect them. However, the thatched roof had been improperly constructed and soon sunlight filtered in between the patches of tall grass. The ray of light struck Gabriella's skin and she burst into flame. Stumbling back, her aflame body caught the rest of the hut on fire. The flames burned bright and licked the thatched roof. Screaming for her, Rain moved in to grab her and get her out of there. The roof came down and sunlight streamed in. His body burst into flames as well.

Pain racking his body, the fire melting his clothes to his skin, he did the only thing he could think of and flew into the sky and landed a moment later into the forest beyond, rolling on the ground to put out the flames. The shade from the dense trees was enough to protect him from the sun's rays, though he still felt the heat of the ultraviolet light dancing on his scorched skin.

Smoke filled the holes in the canopy above, its gray cloud giving aid to protecting him from the sun.

Burned, skin bubbling, he howled against the forest.

Gabriella was dead.

"I still think of you every day," he said softly. "How could I not? I was a part of you and you were a part of me. I miss you."

The tone of Zach's voice when he relayed his memory to Rose carried the same ache that Rain's own voice did on the rare occasion he spoke of Gabriella.

The tone of love.

◆ ◆ ◆

Rose kept her head against Zach's chest. No warmth came from his skin through his T-shirt nor did she hear a heartbeat beneath his breast. If it wasn't for his returned embrace, it would be difficult to tell if she was hugging another person at all.

The sudden sound of his voice echoing through his ribcage sent a jolt through her. "We're not alone."

"I know. I'm here for you," she said, meaning every word.

"No, I mean, we're not alone. There is someone else in the cemetery."

She pulled back from him and glanced out across the graveyard. The gravestones stood up prominent like teeth against the shadowed ground. She couldn't see anything.

"Do you know where they are?" she asked.

"Not yet. But I can hear them. I can hear their boots crunching against the grass."

Amazing, she thought. *The grass is soft, but he hears someone stepping on it as if it is dry.*

Zach stood rigid and the tenderness of their moment together quickly faded. She watched as his dark eyes searched the night, his face a pillar of focus and control.

"The grounds are closed. This isn't a visitor mourning somebody," he said.

Dad. Rose closed her eyes, absorbing the thought. *Please don't find me.*

"Your father?" Zach asked.

She hated that he read her mind, but she couldn't blame him. He probably was still learning to control how and when to search another's thoughts.

"Why would he be here?" he said.

"Looking for me."

"Why?"

His probing was evident. "I didn't tell him I'd be here, but he . . ." Now she'd done it. How could she cover up that her father knew Zach was one of the undead?

"You should go to him," Zach said.

"I know, but I'm scared."

"Don't be. He won't hurt you."

"I know he won't, but" —she smirked— "he'll yell. I'll be grounded, and I probably won't see you for a long, long time."

Zach's eyes still searched the cemetery. "I don't want you to get in trouble."

"What if—" Could it be done? It'd be a huge risk, but might be worth it to help smooth things over. "What if you—Can you put thoughts into someone's head? Like, make them think something?"

"I don't know. Maybe. I'm still learning how to manage that part of me. Only recently did I learn how to block other vampires from reading my mind."

"Can you project it outward? Do you want to try it on me?"

He grimaced. "I can't."

"Why?"

"No time. Your dad is already here, there, one row over. He's peeking out from behind a tree, looking right at us."

♦ ♦ ♦

Mira flew through the air, heading back toward the cemetery. Tonight's feed had been two children wandering around unsupervised in the North End. The area was bad for that, but a blessing to her.

Rose seemed to enjoy herself with us this evening. I sensed everything about that girl. She was so thankful to be around Zach again, to be with his family. I felt her soak everything up and revel in what she herself labeled as a "normal" family life. I can't blame her. Her mother died by Zach's hand—and she doesn't know—

and she's using him to fill the void in her own heart. My Zach, playing two roles and healing the hurt of the girl who lost him and her mother. She smiled. *Perfect.*

The cemetery fence and gravestones below came into view, and soon she saw Zach and Rose standing on top of the family mausoleum. She also saw the slayer eyeing them from behind a tree.

She wouldn't land, but instead would keep high in the tree branches overlooking the mausoleum, out of sight. Quickly, she put up a barrier in her mind to prevent Zach or her husband in the crypt from knowing she was there.

Below, the slayer produced a pair of machetes out from behind his back.

She'd see how it would all play out, and only interfere if necessary.

16

*D*AD, ROSE THOUGHT. "What do we do?"

"I can hear his heart. He's calm. His mind is clear because he knows I can read it. He thinks he's doing the right thing," Zach said.

A shudder ran through her.

"Don't worry. It'll be okay."

What have I done? "I didn't want it to be like this. This is all my fault."

"You're not responsible for his choices."

"But if I hadn't come here, he wouldn't be here and this wouldn't be happening." *It's too soon. Too quick. I just lost myself in all of this and now it's coming apart before it even had a chance to be anything.*

Marcus stepped out from behind the tree. "Let her go, Zach!"

Rose went to speak, but only a small squeak escaped her lips. She looked over the edge of the mausoleum. It was around a fifteen-foot drop. She'd survive if she fell. Might not even sprain or break anything if she landed properly.

"Mr. Jordan," Zach said. "Let's talk. Please."

"There's nothing to talk about, least of all with you. I'm counting to three. Bring her down or I will end you right here," he said.

Rose tugged on Zach's arm. "Please don't hurt him."

"I won't."

"One," Marcus shouted.

"Promise me," she said.

"I . . . promise."

Her dad took a step closer. "Two!"

Rose looked at her father. It was difficult to see him amidst all the shadows. "You hesitated."

"Your safety comes first," Zach said.

"Three!" Marcus retreated into the shadows.

Zach moved with the speed and agility of a cheetah; he grabbed her and pulled her up into the sky. Right after their feet left the ground, a steam bomb struck the roof of the mausoleum and the smell of garlic burst below them. Zach flew straight up faster than the gust of garlic-scented steam could catch up to them. In a large arc, he took her deeper into the cemetery, then gently floated her down amidst a row of identical tombstones, marking the places of those who died during World War Two.

The moment Rose's feet touched the ground, she bent over and put her head between her legs, catching her breath.

"I'm sorry," Zach said.

"It's okay . . . just . . . was caught off guard."

He put his hand upon her back, his touch reassuring. "Stay here. I need to talk to him."

Zach stepped away. Rose shot out her hand and grabbed his sleeve. "No, don't. He'll kill you."

He put his hand on hers. "He won't. I won't let him. But he won't leave us alone until this is resolved. We can work this out. Remember when" —Zach paused for a moment, as if amazed by his own words— "remember when he thought we were spending too much time together? As happy as he was for us, he sat us down and told us to cool it for a bit?"

"You remember that?"

"I do."

"He wanted us to spend less time together so we

could appreciate the time we did have together more."

"He just wants what's best for you, Rose. So do I. I'm going to fix this."

She stood up straight and put her hands on his shoulders. "Promise you'll come back to me."

Gently, he took her hands in his. "I promise." He turned away, then turned back. "I love you."

Hearing those three precious words brought tears of joy to her eyes. "I love you, too."

He took her in with that bold gaze of his, then turned, looked up into the sky, and his feet left the ground.

Rose stood there alone amongst the stones. "Be careful," she said.

Mira looked on from the trees, far enough away from Rose to not be detected. The girl was alone, and would provide the leverage she needed should Zach not be able to hold his own.

To her family in the cemetery she sent a telepathic message: *Stay where you are. Zach needs to handle this by himself. Tonight we will see where his loyalty lies.*

17

Zach flew down, landing not ten feet from Marcus Jordan. When he touched down, he raised his hands in an effort to put the slayer at ease.

"Where is she?" Marcus said.

"She's safe. Still in the cemetery. Just away from us."

"You have no right to take my daughter and do with her as you please."

"I didn't do anything with her, Mr. Jordan. She came here on her own."

"To see you."

"And to mourn her mother."

Marcus grimaced. "Her mother is dead because of you and your kind."

Did he know? Did Marcus somehow figure out *he* was the one who killed his wife? No, he couldn't have. He had no way of knowing. Zach didn't even know that's who she was until the time of the funeral. The brief thought of Mrs. Jordan's death being some kind of setup flashed through his mind, then was quickly interrupted when Marcus said, "What happened to you, Zach?"

"You know what happened to me."

"That's not what I meant, or did you lose your memory in the change?"

"I did, but the more time I spend with Rose, the more I remember who I was and my life before. Who *we* were, Mr. Jordan, you and me. I was hoping to one day be a part of your family."

"You're just a kid."

"A kid who loves your daughter."

"That's exactly my point. You don't remember who you were. The Zach I knew wouldn't speak to me as forcefully as you are now. The power you have, it's made you into something different."

The statement struck a chord with him. How different? So far as he knew, he was the same person, just with holes in his memory. The power of the undead, the gifts, the freedom the lifestyle gave—had he really been transformed into someone new?

"I don't mean disrespect," Zach said. Then, firmly, "I don't."

"You are not the same boy I knew. You followed us home."

"And you're not the same man I knew. You're a slayer, a killer."

"You are the ones who are killers. My job is to protect innocent people from dying at your hands."

Zach kept his hands raised and took a step closer. Marcus drew up his machetes, ready for an attack.

"I'm not going to hurt you," Zach said. "Please. Let's talk this through."

"I know you mean well, and if you do indeed care for Rose and if you do want to protect her, then you'll leave her alone. Her involvement with you will only bring out other vampires and put her life in jeopardy."

"She won't die."

"And turning her isn't an option either, because the girl who she was would be lost in your world of blood and death. I can't let that happen."

The man standing before him wasn't the caring and sometimes overprotective father Zach once knew. All that, it seemed, was just a front to disguise the slayer underneath. The clarity and honesty with which Marcus spoke, coupled with the sincere thoughts running behind it, gave witness that the man now in front him was the man Marcus truly was.

A slayer, born and raised to kill vampires. Everything else was secondary.

"You do realize what you're asking me to do, don't you?" Zach said. "You're asking me to give up the one person I love, the one person who connects me to who I once was, just for you?"

When Marcus spoke, his voice was soft, even caring. "Not just for me. For her. If you truly loved her, if you thought this through, you would see she can't be a part of your world anymore. It won't work."

"I can't live without her, Mr. Jordan." The words came out before he had a chance to catch them.

"You're already dead. You can't feel anything."

"No, you're wrong. I *can* feel. Rose brought that out in me. She's bringing me back."

"You'll always be a vampire."

"But I can be human, too. I was one once."

"And that's just it: *once*. Not now, nor ever again. I'm sorry, but I can't allow it."

Zach moved closer and extended his hands up in complete surrender. "Then kill me now. I don't want to exist without her."

There was a hint of consideration behind Marcus's gaze. Zach searched his mind, but the slayer had shut it and was too well-trained to betray any thoughts to him.

"It's tempting," Marcus said, "but for Rose's sake, I'm willing to let you go on the condition you'll never see her or speak to her again."

"I can't do that."

"Then I will kill you." Marcus moved closer. "Zach, this isn't a joke. Tell me now: will you or will you not leave my daughter alone?"

Rose. I'm sorry. I hope you'll forgive me, and I hope you'll forgive your father for what he's about to do. Zach closed his eyes. "I can't. I love her, Mr. Jordan, and if I'm to die here tonight for that reason, then I gladly lay my life down for her."

Marcus's eyes widened, as if surprised at his answer.

"Once it is done," Zach said, "and if I once meant anything to you as a potential husband for your daughter, then I kindly ask you to tell her I attacked you and you defended yourself. That way, she'll forgive you."

"You want me to lie to her?"

"I want what's best. Now, please, let's finish this." Zach went down on his knees, bent his arms at the elbows, and placed his hands behind his head. "I'm ready."

18

Rose MOVED AMONGST the tombstones, mindful of her footing in the dark, doing her best to stay where the moonlight shone to better negotiate her surroundings. She was too far away to hear any words that might have been exchanged between her father and Zach.

I'm such an idiot, she thought as she ran. *They could kill each other. Dad hates vampires. Hates 'em. Especially after what happened to Mom.* "But why don't I?" The undead had been responsible for her mother's death. Her body, the blood, the removal of the vital fluid that once ran through her—the anger Rose felt after the shock wore off when she first saw her.

She stopped running. Zach had changed her, but not by any conscious effort of his own. At least, not that she was aware of. Besides, he would never control her mind, make her believe something that wasn't true. *Right? I hope so. If he loved me, he wouldn't do that.*

Picking up her pace, she hopped over another tombstone, this one old, gray and weathered smooth from many years sitting in the cemetery.

A dark figure swooped in from the side, planting itself several feet in front of her. Rose stopped. In a blur of motion, the figure darted toward her, for a brief instant seeming to be in two places at once. The nearest one had features: feminine, with long, black hair and a black dress.

Mira.

In a flash, Mira grabbed Rose's arm, gripped it tight, and placed her other hand palm open on Rose's forehead.

"Sleep," Mira said.

Before Rose could react, an overwhelming rush of fatigue clouded her thoughts, made her eyes heavy, and forced the strength from her body.

◆ ◆ ◆

Zach heard Marcus raise a single machete blade into the air. He could only assume in another second his head was going to be removed then, after, Marcus would plunge a stake into his heart and end his life.

Good. If this was going to make things better for Rose, he wasn't opposed.

Eyes closed, there was only darkness, a blanket of chalky black his only sight. As the blade came down through the air, a cloud of inky black encroached across the dark before him, the contrast between the two almost as clear as black and white. In the micro instant before the blade came down, time seemed to slow and a heated rage grew from within, the thirst for blood erasing all other senses. Anger dominated him and he was moving at lightning speed before he even had a chance to register what was going on.

The need to feed.

Survival.

When Zach opened his eyes, he was upright, his hand gripping Marcus's wrist, stopping the blade's descent.

Fire lit up Zach's face as the bones beneath his skin shifted and realigned themselves to prepare to feed. Sharp teeth grew in his mouth, and the black cloud of rage danced at the outskirts of his vision, while everything else took on shades of yellow and red.

In a wild jerk, Marcus raised the hand holding the machete, pulling Zach's hand along with it, setting the vampire off balance. With a swift thrust of his leg, Marcus kicked out and nailed Zach in the stomach. Zach's feet left the ground, then planted firmly back down, never once loosening his grip on Marcus's wrist.

With a hiss, Zach lashed out with his free hand, his claws tearing through Marcus's coat and scraping the armor beneath. He let go of Marcus's wrist, and used that hand to slice the flesh across the man's face, blood gushing out in four distinct spurts.

Howling, Marcus backed away, reached somewhere inside his coat, snapped out his arm, a blur of silver materializing at the motion's end. The silver spike whistled through the air, planting itself deep into Zach's shoulder. With a growl, Zach grabbed the spike and pulled it out of his body. He hurled it back at Marcus, nailing the man's foot to the ground.

With one smooth motion, Zach stepped forward, hooked Marcus across the head, sent the man reeling, then came back up the other side, sending his head jerking the other way.

The slayer grabbed him, drew him in tight in a bear hug, and headbutted Zach before dropping to his knees and yanking Zach's legs out from under him. Zach straightened a second after, only to see Marcus was no longer before him, the stake that had pinned the slayer's foot to the ground now lying in the grass.

From behind, a searing hot pain shook Zach's innards as Marcus plunged something solid and sharp into Zach's back.

"You missed," Zach said, dropped to the ground, and picked up Marcus's fallen blade. He tore the other one out of his back, the wound healing a moment later.

He stood up, brought one blade across Marcus's arm, cleaving off a sliver of meat, then brought the other across the slayer's midsection.

With a screech, Marcus stumbled back, one hand on his middle, the other on his shoulder.

"Curse you," Marcus said through gritted teeth.

Like a lion pouncing on its prey, Zach dove into the air and landed with his feet on Marcus's shoulders. The man collapsed under his weight. With a swift punch to the face, Marcus stopped struggling and Zach positioned himself on top of him.

You can't do this, he told himself. *It's Rose's father.* The darkness around his vision beckoned him on, the hot and bloodthirsty anger driving him kicking into overdrive.

"Just a taste," Zach said. He tore away the collar of Marcus's coat and found the body armor the man wore came right up to the jawline. Growling, Zach gripped the man's head, pulled it up from the ground, then slammed it back down against the earth.

Marcus lay beneath him, limp, face bloody, barely breathing.

"Don't die. Don't die. Need to be fresh," Zach said. He'd bite through the man's skull in behind the ear, then work his way through the bones and muscle and use the neck armor like a soup bowl to get at the main artery beneath.

He suddenly heard his mother's footsteps behind him. She said, "Wake up."

Another female voice groggily moaned. He knew the heartbeat of whom it belonged to: Rose.

The darkness beckoned him to finish the job and drink Marcus's blood.

No. I can't. Not with Rose here. "But if she wasn't . . ." *I can't.* "I can." *No.* "AHHHHH!" Zach jumped off Marcus's body, landed on his feet, and spun around and faced his mother. Mira had Rose in her arms, helping her to stand.

Zach growled. "Why did you bring her here?"

He focused his attention on Rose.

"Zach?" Rose said. She glanced to her father. "What are you—"

"Kill him," Mira said.

His resolve melting away, the beast within yearning to be free, Zach didn't know what to do, what to think. The thirst . . .

"Don't, please . . ." Rose said.

"I . . . I . . ." he said. *Fight it! Fight it for Rose.* To Mira: "I won't. I can't."

Mira put a hand to Rose's forehead. A second later, Rose went limp in his mother's arms. She dropped the girl. Zach was over there in a flash, shoved his mother away, then knelt on the ground beside Rose.

"What have you done?" he asked.

Mira's voice maintained its usual calm. "I have done nothing."

"You brought her here right before I was going to—" He stopped himself.

"Kill her father?"

"Just a taste. JUST A TASTE!"

"You've lost control. Look at you: about to kill the father of the one you love. How pitiful."

He grimaced. "You didn't tell me it was going to be this bad, that the thirst would be so powerful. You've pampered me this whole time. You've lied!"

"No, son, I didn't lie. I guided you. There is a difference. And tonight, you are faced with a choice: do you remain true to what you are and kill the hunter before us, or do you leave him alone for her sake?"

"But why bring her here to see me do it?"

"Her presence reveals your true loyalty. I wanted to see how badly she has corrupted you, and look, even during this short time you had with her, she's made you second guess all that we've taught you to be."

His eyes met hers. The darkness around his vision subsided when he set his eyes upon his mother, but reignited when he looked at Rose's father. *I can't kill a vampire,* he thought.

"No, you cannot," his mother said. "Not one of your own."

"Wake her up!" he shouted.

"Kill her father first, or she will remain that way forever."

"No!"

"Yes. Do it." Mira's visage suddenly changed; her beautiful features melted away, giving birth to a skeletal hag with razor-sharp teeth. She lunged at Zach and shouted in his ear: "DO IT!"

"NO!" He brought his face into hers and bit down, crunching his mother's cheekbones between his teeth.

Screaming, Mira shoved him and pulled away, tearing a part of her face off in the process. She stumbled back, and when she removed her hands from her face, all that remained was tattered skin and displaced bone, all shiny with blood.

Rain, Wil and Cassie appeared from the shadows and came to their mother's side.

"What have you done!" Rain said.

Without answering, Zach scooped Rose up in his arms and took off into the sky, leaving his family, the cemetery, and Marcus behind.

19

Buzzing filled Rose's ears as darkness sat heavy before her eyes.

Faintly, somewhere behind the veil of black, was Zach's voice. *Wake up, Rose. Wake up.* It was more than just words, but an ever-present thought, one that not only saturated her mind, but also, it seemed, her entire being. *Wake up, Rose. Wake up.* The words were familiar, as if she'd heard them from his mouth for a long, long time. *Rose, open your eyes.*

"They are open," she said.

No, they're not. You're sleeping, but you can hear me, which is good. Wake up, Rose. Wake up.

"I can't."

You have to.

Wake.

Up.

Rose.

Wake.

Up.

"Zach? I can't feel my arms, my legs."

You're sleeping. Wake up, Rose. Wake up.

"Stop saying that."

Wake up, Rose. Wake up.

"Stop it."

Wake up, Rose. Wake. Up.

"STOP!"

Her eyes shot open, her vision blurry. What looked like shadow-covered stone was above her. Her arms and legs were pins and needles. A headache pressed in hard at the top of her head. Something else hard materialized against her back, and it was only then she realized she was lying down.

Wake up, Rose. Wake up, Zach demanded.

"I'm . . . awake," she said.

Wake up, Rose. Wake up.

"I said I'm awake!"

Zach's beautiful face appeared upside down over hers as he looked down upon her from behind. "Good. Just wanted to make sure."

"Where are we? Where's Dad?"

"We're in a cave, away from everyone. Something happened that I think you should know about."

About the Author

A.P. Fuchs is the author of many novels and short stories, most of which have been published. His most recent books are *Possession of the Dead*, *Magic Man Plus 15 Tales of Terror* and *Zombie Fight Night: Battles of the Dead*, in which zombies fight such classic monsters as werewolves, vampires, Bigfoot, and even go up against awesome foes like pirates, ninjas, and . . . Bruce Lee.

A.P. Fuchs is also known for his superhero series, *The Axiom-man Saga*, and the author of the shoot 'em up zombie trilogy, *Undead World*. He also edited the zombie anthologies *Dead Science* and *Vicious Verses and Reanimated Rhymes: Zany Zombie Poetry for the Undead Head*.

Fuchs lives and writes in Winnipeg, Manitoba.

Visit his corner of the Web at
www.canisterx.com

Check out the *Undead World Trilogy* at
www.undeadworldtrilogy.com

And follow him on Twitter at
www.twitter.com/ap_fuchs

Did you know **A.P. Fuchs** writes love stories under the pen name **Peter Fox**?

For touching love stories that tug at the heartstrings, look no further than the following:

When a quirky girl named April suddenly sits across from Joseph Bailey at a quiet coffee shop, nothing can prepare him for the weekend ahead and how it'll change him forever.

Jack used to believe in angels.
Her name was Cyan, and they were in love.

Peter Fox books are available in paperback and eBook at Amazon.com or your favorite online retailer.

A.P. Fuchs
Zombie Collection

Axiom-man
The Dead Land
ISBN 978-1-897217-83-2

Blood of the Dead
ISBN 978-1-897217-80-1

Possession of the Dead
ISBN 978-1-926712-53-6

Vicious Verses and
Reanimated Rhymes
ISBN 978-1-897217-95-5

Available at Amazon.com, BarnesandNoble.com
or your favorite online retailer.

Also available through your favorite bookstore.

www.coscomentertainment.com